The Mystery of the Angels

The Mystery of the Angels

Joseph Murphy

LONDON BOROUGH OF EALING LIBRARIES & INFORMATION	
11737650	
Bertrams	04.09.07
	£14.00
19 /STH	HOSP TRANS

Copyright © 2003 by Joseph Murphy.

Edited by: Heather Murphy
              Robert Connolly

ISBN: Hardcover   1-4134-3811-3
              Softcover   1-4134-3810-5

All rights reserved. No part of this book may be reproduced or transmitted in any form or by any means, electronic or mechanical, including photocopying, recording, or by any information storage and retrieval system, without permission in writing from the copyright owner.

This is a work of fiction. Names, characters, places and incidents either are the product of the author's imagination or are used fictitiously, and any resemblance to any actual persons, living or dead, events, or locales is entirely coincidental.

This book was printed in the United States of America.

To order additional copies of this book, contact:
Xlibris Corporation
1-888-795-4274
www.Xlibris.com
Orders@Xlibris.com

22433

Contents

SPECIAL THANKS 15
AUTHOR'S NOTE 17
PROLOGUE 19

PART I - CONQUEST

CHAPTER ONE - ONSLAUGHT 23
Village of Guada

CHAPTER TWO - LA GUERRA DE GUERRILLA 29
Rain Forest North Eastern Columbia
Extraction
Mount Out

CHAPTER THREE - FLIGHT 36

CHAPTER FOUR - BATTLE OF THE BORNE VALLEY 48
Storm clouds
Morning First day
0500 first day
0530 first day
1300 First day
1700 First day
Recon Patrol
0445 Village of Rawa Second day
0530 Company HQ Second day

CHAPTER FIVE - TREATING THE WOUNDED 83
0600 Outskirts of Rawa Second day
0615 Company HQ Second day
0730 Village of Rawa Second day
0540 Village of Rawa Third day

CHAPTER SIX - LOST CONTACT 90
   Regimental HQ Rain Forest Northeastern Columbia
   Isolated

CHAPTER SEVEN - ENCOUNTER 93
   0950 Third day
   1120 Third day
   Road to Meath
   1545 Third day
   1840 Third day

PART II - WAR

CHAPTER EIGHT - KINGDOM OF MEATH 103
   2010 Third day
   0430 Morning Fourth day
   Celebration
   1500 Fourth day
   0445 Mediation Fifth day
   Standing alone
   Decision

CHAPTER NINE - MAELSECHLAINN'S DAUGHTER 127
   Preparing for Battle

CHAPTER TEN - BATTLE OF THE LIFFEY 131
   Dawn Sixth day Blackpool
   Prelude
   Center of the line
   Death of a Knight
   Marine Positions Sixth Day
   0800 Counterattack Morning Sixth day
   Burial with Honors

PART III - FAMINE

CHAPTER ELEVEN - CEAD MILE FAILTE 159
   Late noon

CHAPTER TWELVE - TROJAN HORSE 169
  Struggle
  Wounded
  Medical treatment
  Sweet dreams
  Regimental Compound
  Castle Meath
  Regimental Hospital
  Courtyard Castle Meath
  Springtime

PART IV - DEATH

CHAPTER THIRTEEN - RETURN TO THE PRESENT 193
  Summer
  Regimental Hospital Columbia

CHAPTER FOURTEEN - THE LEGEND 199

EPILOGUE 201

GLOSSARY OF TERMS 203

END NOTES 205

GLOSSARY 209

To my wife's kin, who was the drummer boy with the Irish Brigade, the famed 69th regiment, at Little Round Top at the Battle of Gettysburg on July 3, 1863.

HIGH PRAISE FOR THE MYSTERY OF THE ANGELS

—An intriguing twist of Irish lore
JN
Maine

—Taunting ending
NM
Southbury, Ct

—One would like to believe this could occur
RD
Atlanta, Georgia

—An unbelievable love story; no pun intended
MM
Los Angeles, California

—Time machine revisited with a bit of the Blarney
JK
Brewster, New York

—Ingenious storyline
CP
Miami, Florida

—Author shows a talent for blending factual detail with fiction
JV
Camelback, Arizona

Also by
Joseph Murphy

* * *

Non Fiction

The Wild Geese Trilogy

Volume I: A White Sport Coat and a Pink Carnation
Volume II: Duty Honor Country
Volume III: Valhalla

Fiction

The Mist Series

Volume I: The Mystery of the Angels

SPECIAL THANKS

Writing and completing this book would have been virtually impossible without the help this writer has had from his family and friends. They gave of their time and made suggestions and changes. Each contributed to the whole and as always, some more than others. For their kindness in offering advice to improve this book and establish the series, I want to thank:

My daughter-in-law Heather for reviewing and editing the book;

My daughter-in-law Jodi for the jacket design;

My daughter-in-law Cass for the photography used in the jacket design;

My son Trey, a Major in the Air Force, for reviewing those chapters relating to flight and aircraft;

My son Dan for painstakingly demanding the highest quality;

My son Craig for keeping me up when fatigue and depression set in;

My friend Robert Connolly for also editing the book;

And as always without my side-kick, my wife, the stories would never be written.

Author's Note

Irish Lore is intriguing to say the least. Pick up five different books on a specific subject and you get five different versions. Just as time distances the story teller from the events themselves, so does the repeated telling of such tales. Gradually the stories are embellished in certain areas, honed down in others until they are perfect tales. Not so with Irish story tellers.

The medium of *time* has always intrigued me, especially time travel, because it involves life, death and beyond. This story is based upon a real battle in Irish history in which I have tried to stay with the script; but which one is the real script is any ones guess. I have condensed some of the action, for the sake of clarity, and eliminated some minor characters, for brevity. The battle in question, due to the fog of war, begs for some answers, especially those involving the supernatural. I have attempted to supply those answers by bringing two periods of *time* together and as things would evolve two people together who fall in love. That sets the table for an intriguing ending.

PROLOGUE

The four horsemen of the Apocalypse are described in Chapter six of the Book of Revelation, which is the last book in the Bible. The Four horsemen appear when the Lamb opens the first four seals. As each of the first four seals are opened a different colored horse and its rider is seen by the Apostle John as described in Revelation 6:1-8. The four horsemen are traditionally named *Conquest, War, Famine and Death*.

PART I

Conquest

The first seal is opened: a White horse appears, its rider held a bow it is called Conquest which symbolizes an enemy.

CHAPTER ONE

Onslaught

> Fierce and wild is the wind tonight
> It tosses the tresses of the sea to white;
> On such a night as this I take my ease;
> Fierce North-men only course the quiet seas
> —Ninth/century Irish manuscript

Village of Guada

The hawk, having circled all night, now rose in the new sun, spiraling slowly up and up until the whole valley lay beneath him, with the dark green grass winding down its center and the river Boyne flowing eastward to the sea from the hills. At first the river's course was swift, plunging down to the steep descents of the foothills, but then it slowed as it approached the Irish Sea and eddied there, coursing through caverns at the rivers east end until it surged out in a spectacular cascade, as if from the spout of a great pitcher, to the open sea.

For several leagues southward the road was broad and level. It led straight through the forest along the old flood plain on the west bank of the Boyne, where the trees grew tall and open.

Muirgel happily breathed in that heady Irish mix of heather, sage and broom, spiced here and there with the chimney smoke and the tang of fried herring, as she passed the scattered cottages. The village lay nestled in a small declivity at the foot of one of those soaring crags (steep rugged rocks) that rise so rapidly from the Irish Sea. Those cottages, in the village, near the road were well taken care of, including a new coat of paint.

No one had any hint of terror approaching; no one except Muirgel. Twice during the morning she stopped what she was doing and paused to listen; her eyes suddenly apprehensive, her head turning back and forth across the breeze from the west. No one noticed her. Each time she herself decided she had imagined something, and was soon back giving instructions to her vassals.

There were no walled towns in those days in Ireland; only forts on hills, and a few scattered villages. The population of the country was comparatively sparse. Life, except at the courts of Kings, was simple and primitive. The people were mostly engaged in cattle-raising, and their wealth consisted chiefly of flocks and herds and wearing apparel. The nation was broken up into numerous clans.

In the depths of the river, where fog hung like drapes and swamp gasses sometimes gleaned like spectral lanterns, the oarlocks of boats creaked in the twilight. The Vikings struck as they clambered into stilted huts. Woman shrieked. Men cursed and died, throats gone.

Torches appeared a short distance down the road; Muirgel heard the clatter of hooves and the rumble of wheels coming fast, accompanied by raucous shouting and screaming. Mud caked chariots clattered up at full gallop, scattering dust and sparks from several torches. She heard the terrible rumble of the machines approaching and the snorting of the horses and the bloodcurdling cries of the drivers.

Surprise was complete. Far in the wild, the village had been careless, had posted no guards. Suddenly the attackers, from land and water, were among them, snarling like boars, hacking with daggers, their black capes swarming like separate beasts in the morning sun. Alfrey, a tall slender young man, saw two of his friends go down before they were even on their feet, and another stabbed and knocked back across a fire he was attending.

The Mystery of the Angels

* * *

Chariots were formidable war machines, in fact, the most fearsome antagonist of all. Low, rugged, fast, curved knives flashing on their hubs and the drivers of the chariots knew how to use them. One of the drivers lashing his horses relentlessly narrowed the space between himself and the fleeing villagers. When he came within range, he chose a horrible weapon from the arsenal around him. This was a circlet of polished steel, whetted razor-keen on the outside edge. Driving with one hand, he spun this ring aloft, twirling it with his fingers on the flat inside, and let it go. His aim was perfect as it cut down a young boy in stride. The chariots were upon the fleeing mob and the drivers drew great swords bending low over the side to cut down the panicked villagers. Other Vikings ripped through the village, driving straight for Muirgel. Their frenzy was so strong they were crazed by their blood lust. They slashed and tore at random. The villagers toppled at a blow. People scattered in all directions from the mayhem. Only Muirgel held her ground. As the grizzled warriors bore down on her, the King's daughter standing on a mound of ancient stones grew calm. She stopped screaming. All semblance of order had vanished. All around men died, pinned by lances, hacked by swords, crushed under thrashing hooves. An arrow grazed her side; it drew blood.

Chaos reigned. Dead and dying men littered the village square. The putrid odor of the dead, the roasted flesh, the excrement of horses, the rankness of the marsh; all mingled in a fetid stench in Muirgel's nostrils. She staggered away from the fray, gagging. This was something mindless, something inhuman, something woefully beneath any honorable warrior!

Tuirgeis was mounted on an enormous black stallion. The crimson ensign of his command fluttered from the staff of his standard bearer. A Black cape drifted from his shoulders. Black plate and chain-mail covered his thick torso and his huge legs. Splashes of blood stained his sword and gauntlet. His gaze was riveted on the ongoing slaughter.

"Scum!" he growled "clean them up; kill them all!"

Muirgel turned back to the slaughter. She saw a little child clinging to a burning and collapsing bridge. She saw Tuirgeis striding across the charred bodies of men toward the center of the village where the cries of a terrified infant rang clear. And she saw Iarnkne (I-on-knee), her betrothed, the captain of her personal guard, and his trusted lieutenant Alfrey, hard pressed by a knot of troopers flailing at them with swords and spiked maces.

* * *

The sword arm of the attacker never came down. Knocking aside the shield as if it were paper, Iarnkne plunged his knife into the man's heart. His small band of warriors now at his side kept slashing at their antagonists until there were no more.

One of several adjutants that were with Tuirgeis wheeled his mount and trotted back along the ridge, shouting commands; another adjutant raised a ram's horn to his bearded lips and blew such a resonant, throbbing blast that one felt the very stones quiver under him. Over the rise trotted a legion of fresh cavalry, dressing themselves in battle order as they came. Their horses were of great stature, strong and clean limbed; their gray coats glistened, their long tails flowed in the wind, their manes were braided on their proud necks. The men that rode them matched them well: tall and long limbed; their hair, flaxen-pale, flowed under their light helms, and streamed in long braids behind them; their faces were stern and keen. In their hands were tall spears of ash, painted shields were slung at their backs, long swords were at their belts, their burnished shirts of mail hung down upon their knees When another of the adjutant's sword arm dropped they surged down the slope and over the wretched village survivors; pure blood lust which would turn anyone cold.

Several Vikings had time for only one glancing blow before Iarnkne was among them and they were dying, gripping stabbed bellies, gurgling through slit throats. The quick sword flashed and men died dropped in their tracks or staggered off to die. Smoke and fire all around, he located Muirgel and made off with her.

Tuirgeis' roar of triumph echoed through the village square as he trotted off along the village's edge, hooves kicking up dirt. He gazed on the dilapidated huts and sheds as he passed them. At the far end he wheeled and casually flung his arm out in a gesture done many times. "Burn this place!"

When the last troopers had flung their torches into the village and galloped southward, Muirgel and her personal bodyguard, including Iarnkne, emerged from their hiding place in the woods that they managed to get to during the confusion of the attack. Several of Iarnkne's men were holding horses, muttering soft Gaelic endearments to them amid the smoke and fire. Pyres blazed and ashes smoldered where the small village had been, and smoke hung in a heavy pall over the place. Flames leaped and houses burned causing a smoked arch which enabled Iarnkne to gather Muirgel and urge their horses through. Once mounted they rode hard through the last wisps of smoke; they, then turned their horse's heads towards the valley and safety; a place that always fulfilled Muirgel's dreams. It was rich and fertile, as green as the village of Guada was dark, as abundant as the village of Guada was sterile. Great pastures stretched up the gentle slopes of the mountains, dotted with oak forests and beech trees in the lower regions, fringed with pines and firs toward the top, tonsured around the peaks with the low shrubbery of mountain meadows.

They were mounted and moving before Muirgel had even tucked the layered skirts around her legs, and the material billowed around her like a settling parachute. Iarnkne was silent, but the horses seemed to pick up his sense of urgency, and needing no urging or guidance, they were all but galloping. Still without speaking much, they moved out of the burn and found a comfortable place near the edge of a clearing in the forest. Hills rose in undulant mounds all around them, but Iarnkne had chosen a high spot, with good view of the road exiting the village. The dusk momentarily heightened all the colors of the countryside, lighting the land with jewels; a glowing emerald in the hollows, a lovely amethyst among the clumps of heather, and burning rubies on the red-berried rowan trees that crowned the hills.

Moving parallel to the road, they came down through a narrow, rocky gap between two crags, leading the horses between boulders. The going got easier, the land sloping more gently down through the winding road that led to safety.

Iarnkne dismounted and surveyed the ground, then leaping back into the saddle, he rode upfront of the rest of the party, keeping to one side and taking care not to override the footprints. Then he again dismounted and examined the ground, going backwards and forwards on foot.

"There is little to discover," he said when he returned. "The main trail is all confused with the passage of horseman going back and forth; Tuirgeis' men must have lain nearer the river; but their eastward trail is fresh and clear. There is no sign there of any feet going the other way, back towards Guada. Now we must ride slower, and make sure that no trace or footstep branches off on either side. We want no one to track us."

They turned away from the road to the fords and bent their course northeastward. Night fell, and still they rode on. The hills drew near, but the tall peaks of the mountains were already dim against the blackened sky.

* * *

Muirgel was in pain. The right side of her body was inflamed, puffy, with a foul smelling ooze soaking through the hastily made bandages. Ominous red streaks ran up under her armpit. A bloody wound, she thought to herself; a filthy suppurating, blood poisoning, life-threatening wound. Iarnkne noticed her pain and her red soaked garment.

"We must find a suitable camp quickly to work on that wound of yours."

It was a moonless night, but the starlight caught the metal bits of harness in flashes of quicksilver. Muirgel looked up and almost gasped in wonder; the night sky was thick with a glory of stars such as she had never seen. Glancing around at the surrounding forest, she understood. With no villages now in sight to veil the sky with light, the stars held undisputed dominion over the night.

CHAPTER TWO

La Guerra de Guerrilla

Alert! Alert! Look well at the rainbow.
The fish will rise very soon. Chico is in the house.
Visit him. The sky is blue. Place notice in the tree.
—Operation Pluto

Rain Forest
North Eastern Columbia

The rain forest was still and silent. Its muggy air stank with rot. The midday sun attacked the green canopy above, but the intertwined latticework of foliage allowed only the narrowest shafts of light to dapple the jungle floor. Not even the dripping rain forests and jumbles of rock ridges, in the south pacific, could rival the punishing steeps and tangles of Columbia's rain forests. Jagged mountain peaks always shrouded in heavy mists rose to heights of over 10,000 feet. Beneath them were steep rocky gorges down which turbulent rivers flowed in frothing white rapids, leaping and cascading to the sea in spectacular, roaring waterfalls. Everywhere there was the interminable drip of the jungle. In the rainy season, the downpour was continuous. Trails were nothing more than a primitive track of slippery mud and cruel rock. In some places it climbed the ledges almost vertically. At others it was so narrow that only a single man could pass. Along such a trail that twisted among tall stately trunks of teak and mahogany, Columbian rebels, burdened with heavy packs walked single file.

Everywhere, woody vines hung like thick cables. The men's uniforms were darkened by perspiration and their rifles were slung over their shoulders. If only a squad of them held their weapons ready, Brendan would have let them pass; their carelessness would cost them.

Beads of sweat fell off the brim of Brendan's boonie hat, but he didn't notice. His eyes were fixed on the column of guerrillas coming towards them. He tapped his gunny sargeant lying next to him. Gunny Smith gently pushed back the safety clip of his detonator. Twenty feet away, hidden next to the trail, were deadly claymore mines.

Beads of sweat trickled down Brendan's brow and stung his eyes. He couldn't help but think how young the approaching solders were, probably no more than eighteen; Smith pressed the detonator. The earth erupted in a roaring, shattering explosion of dirt, decayed leaves, jagged plastic and hundreds of steel ball bearings. The lead squad of a platoon of guerrilla soldiers, were violently flung through the air. Their stunned bodies were ripped and torn as if made of paper. Leaves and branches fell like rain into the billowing debris as the green faced men rose and fired. Small arms fire, including automatic weapons, exploded all along the trail as the cries of the dying echoed throughout the valley floor.

Smith pulled his pistol and followed his Captain as he approached the killing zone and the mangled bodies.

Brendan hesitated. The smell—he could never get used to it. It was the odor of plastic explosive mixed with soil and blood, the overwhelming smell of death. He could feel it and taste it.

"Papa Bear, this is Alpha Six," Brendan said, his voice emanating from a handset. "Rebel forces engaged at point of origin right two eight, up zero six. Seven, say again seven rebels killed in action. Five AK-47 and two SKS assault rifles captured in action. No friendly casualties. How copy?"

"This is Papa Bear, Alpha six, good report." The report provided the who, what, where, when, and results. And the results were good. "Good job. Pass along a 'well done' to your men."

* * *

The ambush technique was used with great success, on many occasions. One might think this method of killing as excessively cruel or ugly, but there are several factors to consider: dead is dead, and it makes little difference to the deceased whether his demise was caused by a machine-gun bullet, napalm, or a claymore mine. Moreover the ambush is one of war's oldest tactics and in Columbia it was executed far more frequently by the rebels than the U.S or its Columbian allies.

* * *

Extraction

Brendan spoke into the handset as gunny Smith pulled his map out to coordinate pick up.
"Alpha Six this is Whiskey Echo Zero Three; pop smoke—over."
"Roger."
The CH46 Sea Knights were three thousand feet above the green canopy. Their mission was to pull a squad of Brendan's Marines from their Area of Operations (AO's)."
First Lieutenant Massulo, the lead chopper pilot, pressed the transmit button on the control stick. "I see it! One o'clock."
He banked the aircraft, giving his rear passenger a better view. There it was, a thin column of yellow smoke rising from a small open area.
"Alpha Six, this is Whiskey Echo Zero Three, gotcha stand by."
Massulo flicked the toggle switch on the radio panel, changing to the helicopter channel frequency. "Snake Zero Two, this is Whiskey Echo Zero Three. Over"
"This is Snake Zero Two. Go."
"Take up heading one-zero-eight. I'll pick you up when you're at treetop. Over"

"Roger."

One of the three lift helicopters, Snake Zero Two, and two heavily armed Cobra gun-ships circling an abandoned field at two thousand feet headed south. The pilot of Snake Zero Two could feel the adrenaline flow and smiled behind his green shaded visor as he began his descent. He loved it! He loved buzzing treetops at max speed. All he had to do was fly; and not worry where. The guy above him took care of that. This was what it was all about, he thought, as he leveled off, barely avoiding the top branches of trees passing at ninety knots. Up slightly, then down, following every fold of the terrain below him. Up right, then down. In his excitement his co-pilot was yelling like a bronco busting cowboy at each dip and upward motion. It was a free roller-coaster ride.

"Steer right" Massulo ordered from far above the speeding helicopter. The chopper pilot moved the 'stick' slightly, descended, then pulled back up to avoid a rock face that loomed up ahead, then descended again to the valley floor.

"On course"

He glanced quickly at his air speed and heading.

"One thousand meters"

"Hot damn, baby here we go."

"Five hundred meters"

He could see a trace of yellow smoke ahead.

"Two hundred meters"

"Roger, I got yellow smoke my twelve o'clock." He began his flare. The bird shuttered and dropped.

The right door gunner was leaning out and quickly depressed his transmit button. "Clear right!"

The left door gunner chimed in, "Clear left!"

The co-pilot said matter-of-factly, "Here they come."

The pilot saw nothing as he concentrated on the ground in front of him and gingerly placed the wheels down. The bird hit the ground forty yards away, and the men ran for it at full speed. The screaming engines and whopping blades beating the air were sounds from heaven thought Smith as he leaned into the sixty-knot winds that pushed against him. The door gunner was waving frantically for them to hurry and counted them as the running men jumped into the quivering helicopters—when he reached thirteen he yelled go and all three helicopters took off. The pilots pulled pitch. The stalking gun-ships that had followed them circled once while the three birds made their pickups.

* * *

"Take your seats, gentlemen. The reason I have called you here is to brief you on a major operation that will begin at zero-five-hundred hours tomorrow morning." Brendan Murphy positioned himself beside a large sheet-covered map and picked up a pointer before turning back to face the assembled group.

Brendan pointed toward the map on the wall and raised his voice for emphasis. "A company of Marines must be infiltrated by air, and they must go in undetected. Our assigned area is roughly a rectangle drawn ten kilometers in from this point on the map. He used his pointer to show them precisely where he meant. Based on aerial photos from our micromechanical air vehicles (MAV) and intell reports, we have broken the rectangle down into four squares. The first platoon has the lower quad, the second platoon is in the middle here, and the third platoon has the third quad. Fourth platoon or weapons platoon will be positioned to the right rear of third platoon. You can see the terrain gets progressively denser the farther north we go.

It was 1000 hours, and the small crowded briefing room at the jungle camp was stifling, but the anxious men assembled there didn't seem to notice as they concentrated on the map and their assigned areas. They all knew something big was about to break. Excitement hung in the air like an invisible mist as their stomachs fluttered.

Brendan sipped from his second cup of coffee while looking at the large map blowup of a map of Columbia. Multicolored pins clustered in various locations indicated, Brendan assumed, potential targets, although he never bothered to ask. The young captain was over six feet tall and looked older than his twenty-four years.

"Headquarters wants information about this area." He pointed to the map behind him. "It's all virgin territory; nobody has ever worked it. The river here runs parallel to a major trail we discovered. We will move about 400 meters before coming to this clearing." He pointed to an "X" on the map. "We will move through that clearing to this tree-line directly to the front; move into this valley and then set up defensive positions at the tree-line to the right and dig in; any questions?"

The platoon leaders did not have any.

"Yes sir" responded Gunny Smith. "Once set up, do we act as a blocking force here?" he pointed to the map and Brendan nodded.

"Intel then expects the guerrillas to come from left to right?"

"Yes"

"How long will we be in the area?"

"Four days is usually the max time they'll keep a full company out. That's about all the time the nerves can stand without causing mistakes, and in our business mistakes are forever."

Brendan motioned towards Smith. "First and 2nd platoon has the main trail here and the feeder trail here. You're going in here with the 3rd platoon and weapons platoon on this small tributary that feeds the river. The LZ's (landing zones) are all marked; you can mark them on your maps later."

"That Gunny is a brief overview of how we will operate. Make sure you inform every sargeant down to the finite detail."

"Will do Skipper."

* * *

When Gunny Smith spoke, his voice was always a cranky bark, and his weathered face rarely showed any emotion other than a scowl. The younger Non Commissioned Officers (NCO's) disliked him personally, but professionally he couldn't be beat. That afternoon, each platoon began teaching small squad tactics. Platoon sergeants showed them how to walk point, what signs to look for, what hand signals to give and what ones to respond to. Squad leaders instructed on radio procedures and how to encode and decode messages; Fire-teams taught ambush and search procedures; and reviewed movement techniques, and laagering in a patrol base. The individual Marine had learned it as part of their basic and advanced training, but each line unit had its own way of doing things.

Then that day of reckoning came and immediately someone shouted those hated words:

"Squad leaders, Alpha Company saddle up!"

"Gunny Smith; get these men moving!"

*   *   *

Mount Out

Gunny Smith could hear the familiar sound of approaching choppers.

"Move out!"

With the wind of the Sea Knight's backwash in their faces, they watched the LZ explode in brilliant orange-and-red flashes, each immediately followed by an erupting pillow of black-and-white smoke intermingled with dust, dirt, and bits of foliage and rock, all of which was thrown asunder into Columbia's darkening sky. Smith rose to his knees and nodded at the co-pilot, who was holding up two fingers; then tapped each of his men and alerted them to be ready to disembark. The ground below was a green blur. As the helicopter began its flare, its tail dipped and the blade pitch changed. Smith saw the LZ coming up. The lead Sea Knight slowed, assuming a nose-up attitude, set down and touched the LZ's rocky surface as Brendan's men quickly maneuvered themselves to disembark. They scooted out the rear ramps with the swirling winds biting at them as they exited.

Two at a time the other Sea Knights followed them in, discharging their Marines in a matter of seconds. He looked briefly around at the other choppers and he could see all his men disemboweling from the rear ramps as if being spit out by a giant iron monster.

CHAPTER THREE

Flight

It is well that war is terrible.
We should grow too fond of it
—Robert E Lee
Battle of Fredericksburg

Cautiously, traveling by night, Iarnkne and his party moved north by northwest towards the safety of a village called Rava on the road to the kingdom of Meath. For many hours they rode on through the meads and river-lands. Often the grass was so high that it reached above the knees of the riders, and their steeds seemed to be swimming in a gray-green sea. They came upon many hidden pools, and broad acres of sedge waving above wet and treacherous bogs.

The night chill came on fast, at this time of year, and Muirgel's heavy cloak was barely enough protection against the sudden gusts of icy wind that met them in the open spaces of the clearings. After a few miles they came out onto a narrow road and turned northwest. The way took them up hill again, rising into low, rolling hills that gave way gradually to granite tars and peats. They encountered no travelers on the road, and prudently turned aside into the brush whenever hoofbeats were heard ahead. She was groggy, the damp seeping through the seams of her boots, but she overheard one of her escort raise his voice enough to tell his companions that the night promised to be miserable, especially for such a long ride. As they traveled, Muirgel eyes gradually adapted to the dwindling light, away from the fires, as the horse stumbled through the stones and gorse. She felt the traces of the old road under her horse's feet; the earth packed firm by generations of boots or hooves and trundling wheels. Occasionally there was even a stretch of cobblestones. Where the green grass meandered, the abutments of old bridges still lay among the rushes at the fords. When they left the last vestiges of the road behind, they began to encounter many difficulties. The path wound away from the river into thick forest. Uprooted trees and jumbled rocks had fallen across it, and Iarnkne and group often had to make long and exhausting detours.

Muirgel's wound was now infected and caused her great pain. Iarnkne took pity on her and took off his wrap and flung it over her shoulders. She rode in grim silence, handling the reins with an angry jerkiness quite unlike her usual smooth grace. Several times they stumbled on the sites of ancient battles or ambuscades, where rusting weapons and armor poked out of the roots and where yellowing bones lay strewn like sticks. The vegetation turned to pine forest. They went with as much speed as the dark and tangled forest allowed, following the line of the running stream, northwestward and up towards the slopes of the mountains, deeper and deeper into the woods. Slowly their fear of Tuirgeis died away, and their pace slackened. Muirgel sniffed deeply, enjoying, as best she could, the crisp resinous air, though it was turning chill as the night progressed.

Saddle leather creaking, mail jangling, Iarnkne slowed his mount from a trot to a canter. The horses settled into the slower pace, their breath steaming above their nostrils. It was colder than usual for autumn, promising a deeper winter than the last. It had been a long night's ride, with only a hasty meal eaten in the saddle, and everyone was pleased to stop for a cooked meal. They stopped in a small clearing some way from the path. When they halted and dismounted, even Iarnkne was stiff and weary.

"There's a ford in the stream below," he whispered to her. Sliding down he took both sets of reins and tethered the horses, then gently lowered Muirgel to the ground. One of his men went out and quickly returned dumping his gathering, an armload of sticks, on the ground. At once Iarnkne began busying himself with building a fire. Muirgel then sat down cross-legged on a fold of her cloak, wrapping the rest around her to keep out the chill; while Iarnkne made the fire in a sheltered spot, in a hollow, down among the roots of a spreading hawthorn, tall as a tree, writhen with age, but hale in every limb. When he finished he then moved and sat down next to his fiancée. Muirgel sat in silence with her back to a great tree, deep in thought, as Iarnkne, looked towards the profound shadows of the wood, leaning forward, as one who listened to voices calling from a distance. He then turned towards Muirgel and said "How bad is it?"

"My side is almost numb and I am terribly uncomfortable."

"Bring me hot water, and raspberry leaves quickly," he commanded one of his men.

He then moved closer to Muirgel and proceeded to discard her old bandages, clean the wound by washing it down with the freshly boiled water, as hot as Muirgel could stand it without burning the skin. Without sulfa drugs or modern antibiotics, heat was the only defense against a bacterial infection. Muirgel's body was doing its best to supply that heat by means of high fever, but the fever itself posed a serious danger, wasting muscle and damaging brain cells. The trick was to apply sufficient local heat to destroy the infection, while keeping the rest of the body cool enough to prevent damage, and sufficiently hydrated to maintain normal functions. He then rewrapped new bandages around the wound.

Muirgel made a feeble attempt to assist with the cooking, but her help had more or less been politely rejected by the taciturn individual whose job it apparently was. After the meal and fatigued from the night's ride, they scooped together a nest-like wallow of pine needles and blankets and huddled close together for warmth as they cast themselves on the ground and all at once fell asleep, except for Iarnkne who stood guard. It was chilly, and he wrapped his cloak about him. The moon was shining cold and white, down into the dell, and the shadows of the bushes were black. All was silent, and there was no sign or sound of living thing. The night was barred with long clouds, fleeting on a chill wind. The night grew ever colder. Muirgel slept fitfully, and whenever she awoke she saw Iarnkne standing beside her, or walking to and fro, talking softly to himself and as he talked the white stars opened in the hard black vault above; the night passed.

Before dawn was in the sky they woke and rose. Everyone behaved as usual, if moving a little more stiffly from the effects of fighting and sleeping on rocks. Muirgel appeared still deep in slumber, and Iarnkne was still standing, gazing northwest into the darkness, thoughtful and silent as a young tree in a windless night. North-westward stalked the dark forest surrounding the village of Rawa.

"There is danger about," said Muirgel in a low tone, as she woke.

"I agree," repeated Iarnkne "we must move before first light."

"Why didn't you just leave me?"

"Leave you? What are you saying?"

Iarnkne put a hand to Muirgel's lips to stop her questioning and his gull-winged brows rose in a graceful arc of inquiry. "Are you questioning my honor? Do you think for one moment I would leave you? Why I would gladly exchange my life for yours. Therefore, tell me why honor is not a suitable exchange for your life?" The brows drew together in a scowl and in a softer voice. "Or are you telling me that I may not love you as much as you love me? Because if you are Muirgel, I'll tell you right now, it's not true!"

Muirgel opening her mouth to reply before he was finished was taken at a loss by his conclusion. She closed her mouth abruptly as he pressed his advantage. She had said the wrong thing, she knew, but she was too proud to apologize; or maybe just too embarrassed. She had really hurt him. She could tell by the look in his eyes and the tone in his voice.

Muirgel had seen the determination on Iarnkne's face and knew arguing with him was futile. She knew that she was in serious trouble. The infection in her side and up her arm was spreading. She was growing weaker and becoming more and more a burden to Iarnkne and his men. She put them in grave danger.

Iarnkne's hard gaze slowly softened. "You know Muirgel," he said, "You should always keep your chin up." He smiled warmly, looking deep into her glistening eyes "Because I do love you, even though you are thick-headed, at times. And I will not have you dead at my feet because you are too stubborn to keep your mouth shut for once in your life! Now you will eat something."

* * *

They went on once more, riding swiftly. Hours passed and still they rode on. Muirgel was stiff in every muscle. Iarnkne had a handful of oats in a small bag on his saddle horn, and forced her to eat some oats mixed with cold water. It stuck in Muirgel's throat, but she choked it down.

Twelve leagues now lay between them and their destination; the village of Rawa. Beyond there glimmered far away the last peak of misty mountains. Muirgel nodded at one point and would have fallen from her saddle, if Iarnkne had not clutched and shaken her.

Following with his keen eyes the trail to the river, and then the river back towards the forest, Iarnkne saw a shadow on the distant green, a dark swift moving blur. He cast himself upon the ground and listened again intently. It was not a blur, but the small figures of horsemen, many horsemen, and the glint of morning on the tips of their spears was like the twinkle of minute stars beyond the edge of mortal sight.

Evil and death, death and Evil; the two mingled as palpable as smoke in that foul forest; and they were glad to leave it behind.

A gust of wind screamed down the slope of the rolling hills in front of Muirgel. It tore across the plain toward her, through copses (thickets) of white barked birches along the way. Already stripped of their leaves by the season, the trees rattled, woody skeletons. A bitter cold chill came into the air. Slowly in the east, the dark faded to a cold gray. Red shafts of light leapt above the black walls far away upon their left.

In a pattern made familiar over the past hour, Muirgel turned in the saddle to relieve the pain from her wound. The moment she shifted her mare's head came up, her mane and tail streaming.

Muirgel hunched her shoulders and waited for the pain to subside. The stinging pain penetrated her woolen cloak; then passed through her tunic as if the garments didn't exist. Her hood fluttered around her cheeks, straining against the scarf tightly wound around her face to keep the hood over her eyes. It was to elude any of Tuirgeis' scouts that they had taken the least direct and longest path to Rawa.

A wind swept across their path, rushing through the bent grasses. The first light of morning was now beginning to strain the darkness on the other side of the mountain when they came upon a river and suddenly stopped. The morning was bright and clear about them, except for isolated patches of clouds and mist, and the birds were singing. The river ran down swiftly into the plain, and beyond the feet of the hills turned across their path in a wide bend, flowing away east. The wind rattled through the dead brambles like the passing of a deer's ghost, still in panic flight from the hunter.

"What is it?"

Muirgel could see nothing through the mist, to their front, despite the patches of early sunlight that mottled road and field. There was a pine grove up ahead, and the horses seem disinclined to go any nearer to it. She strained her eyes and ears to discern whatever it was still troubling the horses; they shifted and stamped ears and tails twitching in agitation. The clouds by now had shredded and flown on the early morning wind, leaving only scattered trails across the face of a brilliant sunburst. In spite of the growing brightness, she could see nothing on the road ahead, or in the menacing grove.

The grove was dark, but not still. The pines roared softly to themselves, millions of needles scouring in the wind; very ancient trees, pines, and eerie in the gloom. Gymnosperms, cone-bearers, winged—seed dispersions, older and sterner by far than the soft-leaved, frail—limbed oaks and aspens.

At last, they heard a faint, confused shouting from the direction directly in front of them. One of Iarnkne's men put a hand on the bridle of Muirgel's horse and motioned toward the shelter of the trees.

Two warriors appeared out of the thinning mist. Lances and bows were slung over their packs like slender horns. Iarnkne's joy at the return of his friends, including Alfrey, was perfunctory compared to his delight when a warm fire finally began to blaze. Muirgel bedraggled, muddy, and weary, slumped against a tree. She was modestly covered by her bloody soaking gray cloak as she lay back watching the small fire crackle sending its red and gold sparks upward into the morning light. A cold chill ran through her body. The air was cold and heavy, away from the fire. Her shirts were damp from sitting on the ground, and clung to her legs. Iarnkne could see her profile, lips pale and set with chill.

"Are you hurt, then? Just a bit scratched? Well, you're cold no doubt, and a little bit shaken, I imagine. Sit over here closer to the fire. I will have Alfrey fetch you something, and then you can tell me a bit more about the wound." Iarnkne pulled a small log over and sat firmly on it with a massive hand on Muirgel's shoulder.

Small wood, with peat, fires give a little light but are comfortably hot. Muirgel shuddered involuntarily as the blood started to flow back into her cold hands.

"Next time I will make sure I tell you I heard something."

"You need something hot, lass," Iarnkne said matter-of-factly, "and a bit to eat as well. Something in your belly will help more than anything." she laughed shakily at his attempts to pour broth one-handed, and attempted to help. He was right; food did help. They all sipped broth and ate bread in a companionable silence, sharing the growing warmth and fullness.

At a nod from Iarnkne, one of his men gently pulled back Muirgel's garment, next to her side, revealing a dirt smeared linen blotched with blood. A small man with a thick mustache came up behind her with a single-bladed knife, and holding down the linen, slit it across the side and down the hip, so that it fell away from her side. He gasped as did several of the men. The wound in her side was a deep, ragged furrow across the top, and blood was running freely down Muirgel's side. They moved to patch it and stop the bleeding.

Finally Alfrey stood up and a hand vanished into the folds of his cloak and reappeared holding a small leather flask "Whiskey, anyone? No? Well then . . ." He took a swig, tapped the stopper back in and smacked his lips.

Someone passed the flask to Iarnkne and Muirgel could smell the hot burnt-smelling liquor as he drank. She wasn't at all thirsty, but the faint smell of honey reminded her that she was still starving and hurting. Even though she had broth and bread her stomach gave an embarrassing growl, protesting her neglect. Moments later, a hand with a flask came around in front of her again.

"Better have a little nip" Iarnkne whispered. "It will not fill your belly but it will ease the pain somewhat and make you forget you're hungry."

"Are you sure?" Muirgel uttered. "Will that help?"

"Better than you can imagine my Lady" Alfrey replied with a grin.

Once the searing effect of swallowing the stuff passed, it did induce a certain spurious calmness.

She tilted the flask and swallowed. A couple of more gulps from the leather flask and it started the blood flowing internally again as well. With considerable presence Alfrey put a hand behind Muirgel's neck and pressed the flask to her lips. She winced as the spirit stung her mouth, but drank thirstily from the beaker before laying her head down again. Her eyes slanted up at Alfrey, slightly filmed with pain and whiskey but alight with amusement nonetheless. He then placed a hand on her head, turning it to inspect a large bruise over the cheekbone. "You look bloody awful. How do you feel?" He asked, from force of long-held habit.

"Alive." She struggled up onto one elbow to accept with a nod a second flask of whiskey from Alfrey's companion.

"On second thought, I don't think you should drink too much all at once." Alfrey stated looking into her eyes for signs of concussion.

Muirgel thought that right now she'd like nothing more than to drink until she could drive the past twenty four hours from her mind.

"I agree that will be enough for the present, Alfrey," said Iarnkne, reappearing from the fire "She needs hot strong tea and sleep, not more whiskey."

* * *

With Muirgel once more seated atop her spavined mare, they left the site to make their way northward toward the village of Rava, from there to Meath. All around Muirgel, trees swayed in the wind, their naked branches rattling. Fallen leaves, their autumn brightness giving way to the mottling of cold and damp, danced around her, skittering across frostbitten grass. She was a little warmer today and it wasn't just Iarnkne's cloak that made her feel this way. She was fevering from the wound. She shut her eyes for a few seconds then quickly opened them as the pain grew worse.

Alfrey had been correct the whiskey built a small warm fire that burned comfortably in her stomach, obscuring the hunger pangs and the pain from the wound. She managed without incident for several miles, taking turns with both reins and the whiskey flask.

* * *

Looking across the burn, Muirgel's eyes were dazzled by the morning sun blazing through the cold mist on the far bank. Her heart began to beat faster. The village of Rawa and its distinctive castle rose ahead. Its gray stone tower, unlike its walls, soared high enough to pierce the sky. It was the most magnificent structure Alfrey had ever seen. Built of the same marble as the road, it glowed so pure and white under the rising sun that it seemed a source of light itself. A tower rose from within the structure like a welcoming beacon beside the lowered flagstaffs. Sunlight briefly flashed on the silver surface of the moat which surrounded it; as gray clouds moved in.

When the wind drifted past Iarnkne, this time the faint scent of wood-smoke and penned livestock filled its depths; the promise of civilization lie ahead on this track. A little further on, grassy pastureland gave way to cultivated fields. The scars, left upon the earth by plows, ran at odd angles, plot by plot, as each family strove to take the best advantage of drainage and sun angles. Depending on the reek Iarnkne could tell which of the fields would rest beneath a layer of manure for the next season. The village of Rawa which owned the plots appeared to be of small size, several hundred dwellings.

Saddle leather still creaking, and their mail jingling their party slowed their mounts from a gallop to a trot. As Iarnkne drew another angry breath, he again caught the scent of wood-smoke. That scent brought with it the promise of security, warmth, and food. They slowed their horses to a walk.

Iarnkne also slowed his horse from a canter to a walk so the gelding could catch its breath. While they walked, he glanced around him. His horse was trembling beneath him, his sides heaving. Iarnkne shoved his hand back into the glove, he had previously removed. He flexed his fingers once, to gauge how much damage was done to them in the fight at Guada. From near the top of this latest rise, the cottages in the distant village looked like children's toys. There were a few dozen homes, every one of them shuttered against the weather, their front and back gardens sleeping for the season beneath a blanket of straw. Cattle and sheep stood like dark dots against the empty sweep of open pastureland, while the long expanse of fields that fed them and their stock flowed like rich black velvet over the sweep of the landscape.

There was no welcome. The closer they came the more Muirgel's joy and relief shifted to foreboding and unease. No birds sang in the trees through which they rode. No animals moved in the fields and forest. Although a breeze coursed through the valley, the King's banner did not flutter on its staff. Her pain grew worse. She was exhausted, her garments were sodden, her fingers and toes so cold she couldn't feel them. She was going through spasms of hot and cold flashes. Stewing in uncertainty, Muirgel clung to her horse and waited as Iarnkne brought his mount alongside her. Wisps of steam floated up from her horse's hide and clouded in front of its nose as it huffed against exertion. Iarnkne wore his sword belted at his side. His scabbard was black. A bit of silver tracery ran down its center to a solid silver tip; modest embellishment, given his violent and skillful repute. More often, the greater the warrior's renown, the gaudier the decoration on the tools he used to maintain his fame.

Iarnkne pulled down the scarf that covered his face. His eyes glinting silver, might have been carved from stone. The wind rose in intensity, howling around them. The fur inside his cloak ruffled, the end of his scarf lifted. His horse's mane streamed across his gloved hands on the reins. Iarnkne bent his head into the autumn wind, a mix of cold mist and frigid air. Riding in next to him Muirgel curled as close as she could to her horse's body. Her head was tucked to the left side of the horse's mane. She pulled as much of her cloak around her as she could, yet the autumn air radiated through her. She shivered so violently that Iarnkne worried about her. They jolted along for a couple of hours in this manner, but the pain grew steadily worse, keeping her shifting in the saddle incessantly. She simply must get off for a while.

"Whoa!" she said to the horse and swung down gingerly. The rest of the party came to a halt.

Stripping off his gloves, Iarnkne tucked them into his belt, than touched a hand to Muirgel's cheek. His fingers were warm against her chilled skin. The corner of his mouth lifted as he freed a quiet breath. "In all my days I never thought to hear myself say this to any woman, but especially to a gentle woman. I cannot bear the thought of losing you." His voice was gentle as his fingers moved against her cheek in a sweet caress.

His words of love brought a smile to Muirgel's pale lips. She was sinking into unconsciousness as she sighed and leaned her head into his caress.

"Nor do I wish to lose you," she told him at a whisper. The thought of him was a leaden weight in her mind, a pendulum swinging slowly at the end of a rope. The road appeared to continue endless and dreary before them.

Once remounted, the animal pens appeared on Iarnkne's right, nestled at the place where a hill rose from the base of the plain. It was more distant from the path than he expected, which was a boon, indeed. As they neared the pens, he saw that the chest high fences were made of willow branches woven into a wall. They were efficient enclosures for a Shepard. Being both flexible and portable, the pens could be moved, rearranged or rewoven as needs demanded.

Muirgel smelled the village before she actually saw it. The chill wind brought her the ever-present scent of wood smoke, only here, as with every other pocket of humanity, the stench of village life, the reek of offal both human and animal, twined with that homely scent. The distant, frightened bellow of some dying oxen rang out, no doubt from the town's shambles as the butcher made his last slaughter of the day. The pain grew stronger.

The Mystery of the Angels

The village's main gateway appeared to their right. Like its walls Rawa's gate towers were constructed of wood, a far less impenetrable substance than stone. But then this wasn't much of a village, what with less than four hundred inhabitants. Their panic had its roots in a site some hundred yards in front of the main gate where it appeared a battle had taken place. Torn by iron-shod hooves, great gouts of sod had been strewn across the grassy clearing, those earthy chunks testifying to some sort of violence. Patches of flattened and darkened grass suggested men had laid upon them and bled. Muirgel's only comfort, and it was cold comfort, indeed, was that she'd seen no ravens or crows circling anywhere near the site. Those carrion eaters were the scourge of the battlefield. Drawn by the sound of clashing weapons, the fearless creatures didn't even wait for the fighting to end or death to claim the victims before feasting on the fallen.

CHAPTER FOUR

Battle of the Borne Valley

> A war of gigantic proportions, infinite consequences,
> And infinite duration is upon us, and will affect the interests and
> happiness of every man, woman and child, lofty or humble, in this country....
>
> —John M. Daniel
> Richmond, Virginia, 1861

Storm clouds

The sound of morning arriving, settled over the valley. Birds of various varieties started their clamor. A fog from nowhere was slowly moving in from the west as the sun was doing battle with the morning dew. The chatter of the birds was reaching a crescendo when it suddenly stopped. There was tension in the air. It was almost a living presence. The morning had grown ominously black. Rumbling thunderheads moved in from the south, and strange winds came scudding up the valley, like swirling clouds. The stillness was deafening; and then suddenly movement covering a wide front in the bush was discerned. Then slowly very perceptively, dark figures, row on row, long, long rows, like walking trees, coming out of the dew, could be detected moving in camouflaged crouched positions as they broke from the tree-line. Marines, several hundred of them, were moving in a skirmish line from left to right.

"Alpha three, this is six, stay on line; you are falling behind. Do you copy?"

"Alpha six, read you loud and clear."

"Alpha one this is six, slow down and let the others catch up."

"Roger six, I copy."

* * *

The Marine Company commander, a tall young muscular captain, looked around, held up his hand for all his platoon leaders to see and then gave a "palms down". The line of men halted and immediately went to the ground. The sky was becoming overcast, and a thin fog, which hung in the air like a mist, seemed to be rising from the ground. It was a fine mist-like rain that was blowing, cold and clean, in the soft valley air. An occasional slant of early morning sunlight would find its way through the clouds and tree branches, and turn the mist to smoke.

The Marines were midway to the next tree-line, which lay about five hundred yards to their direct front. There was a slight valley or opening in the middle, when the mist became heavier. The mist moved through the long grass like fingers through hair. It continued to roll from left to right and as it picked up speed, visibility decreased. A darkness rushed by as the wind sang loudly in their ears.

The captain turned to his gunny sergeant and told him "Gunny, I have a funny feeling; get me the platoon leaders, I want a meeting right now, right here."

"Yes Sir!"

There was an odor of trouble, an indefinable wrong. In the distance were the drums of thunder. The sky above and to the west was now dark with thunder, and lightning far away flickered among the tops of hidden hills. It was like playing chess and making a move, and not knowing why, but knowing instinctively that it was a bad move. Lightning flickered through the sky. The instincts were yelling; as they used to do long ago at night in 'Indian country'. Brendan, his back to his immediate front, gazed out into the mist waiting. His fame as a poker player was legendary but he had not played in a long time, and he did not feel like it now; especially with the lives of his men. He looked down and every important part of his equipment was tied to his person. One glance at the compass confirmed his map bearing. He reoriented the map, placing the compass straight edge along the grid lines superimposed on the map. Looking at his map, he knew the terrain would slowly descend and abruptly drop off into a large valley about five hundred meters away. They would move west and eventually run into a large, well used trail that paralleled a river.

* * *

A few minutes later, they were all there. In that misty light, Brendan had assembled his platoon commanders. His carriage was stiff, his jaw square, and his glance struck straight from narrowed eyes. They were silent, watching him. The young captain had that hard to define yet unmistakable aura of command. He was used to giving orders; and used to having them carried out. In the moist and misty setting at his improvised command post, the Marine company commander described the general situation to his officers and candidly told them what little he knew about the terrain ahead. The soft-spoken commander possessed a quiet, gentlemanly demeanor that radiated both optimism and determination. He had received a four-year football scholarship to college and played with an intensity and devotion that made him well known and respected. His reckless style and his total self-confidence were overpowering to men and woman alike. The flash of his dark brown eyes and his brief, ironic smile were charismatic, and yet, there was always a strange cold reticence about him that sometimes made him seem inaccessible. As captain of the football team he was able to demonstrate his innate qualities of leadership: his zest, his devotion to the ideal of teamwork, his unflagging interest in the intricacies of what is certainly the most complicated team sport in existence, his capacity for hard work, and his ability to get the best from his players.

Life to Brendan Murphy was to be met head on. It was no surprise to anyone that his body was firm and well muscled. His brown hair was brush-cut short. Life's barriers were not to be gone around; he preferred to go through them, to feel the power of conquering obstacles the difficult way. His nose had been broken twice once playing football, the other time on the baseball diamond. His style of play even raised baseball from a non-contact game to a collision sport. It was a strange satisfaction, and it drove him to even more barriers. His four years of college provided many; the studies, the varsity football team, the women, were all slowly, methodically, conquered.

At some time during school there came an empty loneliness. His successes became hollow. He began a search. It ended when he realized that he was a lot like his father and that deep down he wanted to be like his father, a Marine. He joined the Marine Corps the day of graduation.

* * *

"Gentlemen, this pea soup is getting worse; I don't want anybody to get lost much less walk into a bunch of trouble, so we will hunker down right here, until this strange fog blows away. Also, I want the 1st platoon and 3rd platoon on my flanks to bow the line. I don't want to be surprised on my flanks. Weapons platoon, because of the terrain, will be in reserve behind and slightly to the right of 3rd platoon. Do I make myself clear?"

Everyone looked at each other and then slowly the soft chorus came from the four butter bar Second lieutenants. "Yes sir"

The Marine commander's company was responsible for defending a 900 yard front. Two of the rifle platoons, 2nd and 3rd platoons, led by second lieutenants Robert Mastrion and Bruce McMillan, respectively, manned the front and right flanks. Two platoons, the 1st and weapons platoon led by John Nichols and Anthony Roberts, would be dug in along the left flank and on the extreme right flank in the rear. As he spoke the young captain felt a shift in the wind and glanced up at the sky. The light, fluffy clumps of clouds that had been there earlier were now massing into something large and dark; and away to his right, vast shadows in the sky marched past. Although he was in supposedly "friendly territory" he didn't want to take a chance on one of his Marines being hit by lightning. The sky was utterly dark, and the stillness of the heavy air foreboded some sort of a storm. As he signaled his lieutenants to go back to their respective platoons, the first rumble of thunder shook the ground. Suddenly the clouds were seared by a blinding flash. The butter bar lieutenants' slow pace was replaced with frantic haste as they rapidly made their way back to their respective platoons. There was a sudden flash close at hand, with the crash of thunder following close on its heels, the sky opened and poured down on them.

"Move it! Move it!" cried the company commander. "It's going to get worse!"

The second ripple of thunder shattered the sky above them. Branched lightning smote down upon them. Brendan turned to his gunny sargeant and gave him a look knowing that they were all going to be soaking wet before they got back to their destinations. A strong gust of wind blew a curtain of rain against the back of his legs. Turning his mind to more pertinent affairs, he quickly covered himself in his nylon poncho liner. It was light as a feather to carry, but if a Marine could wrap up in it and stay out of the overnight, his clothes would be dry by morning.

The trees rattled as the thunder continued to rumble and the lightning began to flash. The rain grew worse and they could not even move in under a tree because of the lightning. Water poured from skies so dark that the forest became a murk of gloom. The gunny set his eyes on Brendan Murphy and focused on the sound of his skipper's voice. Brendan had a square face that offered a fine bone structure and a strong chin. He was well built, handsome, and a deep commanding voice; all the qualities of a leader.

As the storm raged darkness turned daylight into night and didn't allow much visibility. Wind-whipped trees bent low to the ground, their branches bowing in supplication to the greater strength of the storm.

Just before complete darkness descended upon them, a great shaft of lightning came down from the sky, a blaze of yellow fire behind dark barriers; shattering trees as it pierced the wood-line. To the mud-Marines it seemed they would never be dry and warm again. The rain soaked through their ponchos; their inner garments were already damp and sticky.

Storm clouds had come quickly and gunny Smith was starting to get nervous. Gunny Smith was a craggier looking man. He had dark hair striking hazel eyes and a clean face. His chin a bit squarer, cheeks leaner, features more jagged. He had good eyes, though; a strange shade of hazel that made them amber at times, almost gold at others. One of his men once said he had a sense of humor so small that it could have danced on the head of a pin. At best guess, the Company was moving directly into the storm's path and that was not wise; but the skipper was right to keep the outfit in open country rather then in the tree-line. Just thinking about the thunder and lightning gave him a feeling of sick lassitude; but what really bothered him was this strange mist that was upon him.

Lieutenant Anthony Roberts, the weapons platoon commander, was trying to bury himself deeper into his freshly dug fox-hole but rain was everywhere, seeping through the walls and coming up through the floor of his fox-hole. The ground beneath his feet began to give, and he felt himself sinking. He struggled futilely to hang on to solid ground. Thunder again sounded, rolling throughout the heavens above his head and sapping his strength to move. Water was rising in the hole to his knees, soaking his boots and the calves of his fatigues. He pulled half of his poncho over him to keep him as dry as he could.

Lance corporal Henniger hunched over, trying to keep the rain out of his cold Lurp (food rations). Water trickled down his chin as he spoke to the gunny. "No aircraft up in this shit, huh?"

Gunny Smith, or Smitty to some, sighed heavily. "No, probably won't be until this stuff breaks, but this would be a good time for the guerillas to move."

Henniger tried to control his shaking hand as he brought a spoonful of the cold food up to his mouth. "Yeah," he took the bite and chewed a moment. "They could move a whole division in this crap and we couldn't hear them much less see them."

* * *

Night fell swiftly, the rain slackened, and then it was black and silent except for the small sounds made by the creatures that move at night. The night darkened and the stars had disappeared. One by one the men wrapped themselves in their wet ponchos and tried to sleep. In the stillness of the night, sound was always amplified and it made sleep difficult, because it was hard to distinguish between animal, friend and possible foe. Few animals were to be seen or heard in the forest. Unlike foolish humans, they would not venture from their dry shelters.

Those on watch could see flashes of lightning over the horizon as the downpour continued. The forest seemed to flow around them like a silent dark sea. At night, the Marines lay still in their holes, peering into the rain-swept darkness.

* * *

Morning
First day

The light of day was straining to break through in the sky, and O'Hare, a tall lanky leatherneck, roused himself and looked up. He was six two, broad-shouldered and narrow hipped. His square jaw and deep, piercing brown eyes made him seem older than his twenty years. To his left lay a sea of mist, rising to a bleak shadow in the west; but to his right large hills reared their heads, ranging from the east to a steep and sudden end, as if in the making of the land the river had burst through a great barrier, carving out a mighty valley. When it was not raining or misting, moisture seeped up from the muddy forest floor. The fog shrouded the valley before him.

Gunny Smith woke to the sound of voices. The men of Alpha Company First Battalion, First Marines rose from their watery sleeping bags, it was twilight: the cold dawn was at hand again, and gray mists were still about them. Heavily laden Marines, with weapons were moving about.In front of them in the mist loomed the tree-line. The sound of weapons being checked could be heard. Machine gunners went over long belts of ammunition coiled wickedly in oblong green boxes, carefully withdrawing and reinserting the cartridges into their loops, making sure they would not stick and jam the guns. Other men adjusted packs, inspected grenade pins or rearranged camouflage nets for their helmets

Thick gray clouds trailing their black shadows across the valley floor chased the clear sky beyond the horizon. The sun flashed an occasional quick shaft of light towards the green hill in the distance. Despite the thick pungent smell of grass in the August air, the Marines shivered with the cold wetness from the previous day.

Corporal O'Hare sat quietly for several minutes, not thinking about much of anything as he waited for the company to move out. He listened for the sound of animals chattering away somewhere in the branches of the tree-line to his direct front; but the woods were almost completely silent now. The birds were not even singing for some reason or other. O'Hare wondered if that might be symbolic. O'Hare was a natural. He was one of those types that men like to be around, a man's man, tall, good looking, broad-shouldered, athletic, very classy yet personable. Not temperamental but calm and always in complete charge. He had a presence about him that put people at ease. And as a leader, he was good; a real professional who asked nothing of his men that he wouldn't do. He also liked his skipper. That judgment had been made as soon as the captain expressed concern over the well-being of his men. He hadn't had to do that but it was obvious he cared for his men. His type was rare. Caring was not a prerequisite for leadership, but O'Hare felt sorry for the men who only played at the game of leadership; the ones who mouthed the proper platitudes, accomplished the missions, took the glory, but never really knew the men who made the successes possible. Such leaders never really got the respect or loyalty they wanted from their men.

Joseph Murphy

0500
first day

The officers began to assemble the men as instructed the day before. The Marines were a sorry—looking lot with blood shot eyes, unshaven faces and dirty fatigues. They had been chasing guerrillas in Columbia now for the past four weeks with little or no sleep. The heavy mist still obscured their view of the tree-line. Nevertheless, according to marching orders, Murphy deployed his two hundred and forty four Marines of Alpha Company, First Battalion, First Marines. As they jumped off, they made an almost perfect skirmish line towards the wood-line; five hundred yards across an open and level field covered with beautiful green grass six inches high. On the left was the 1st platoon, in the center the 2nd, and on the extreme right flank the 3rd platoon. Headquarters section and the heavy weapons platoon pulled up the rear. What was not known, because no reconnaissance was made due to the strange mist, was if the woods directly to their front were occupied or empty. The terrain object before them was an elongated stretch of land rising above the valley they were in. It was more like a large finger pointing northward with a sharp drop on each side. As Gunny Smith trotted along through the foggy mist, he felt his canteen bumping against his hip and smelled the dampness of the grass under his feet. He glanced to his left and then his right at the determination on the faces of his men with their rifles at the high port position as they advanced in mass. They were mostly boys in their late teens and early twenties. Though they were high-hearted volunteers, tough and sturdy youths who had flocked to the Marines in the weeks following the World Trade Center attack, they were barely better than "boots." Recruiters had worked through the nights following September 11, 2001 to process the astonishing throngs who flocked to sign up. Red cross ladies were there passing out free doughnuts and coffee, and cots had been set up for those wearied by standing in line or those needing to sleep off the kind of patriotism that sometimes comes in bottles. These young men and woman came from all over the country. They represented every race and creed that had emerged from the American melting pot as Yankees. They were to a man or woman mad. Their country had been treacherously attacked and they were angry. They spoke of the terrorists in terms that were neither complimentary nor printable. They had been in Afghanistan and Iraq, and now they were assigned the task of eliminating the terrorist guerilla organization known, in Columbia, as the Revolutionary Armed Forces of Columbia "FARC". From all over the Marine Corps, the old salts were returning to active duty. There were NCOs yanked off soft duty at the navy yards, there were the grizzled old gunnery sergeants—the schoolmarms of Marines— who had fought in Somalia, Bosnia and the Gulf War I. There were the professional privates who had spent as much time in the brig as in barracks. Gamblers, drinkers and connivers, brawlers in starched, creased khaki and natty "piss-cutter" caps, they had fought sailors and soldiers of every nationality in every bar from Brooklyn to Bangkok; blasphemous and profane with a fine fluency that would astound a London cockney, they were nevertheless dedicated leathernecks who knew their hard calling in every detail from stripping a machine gun blindfolded to tying a tourniquet with their teeth. They were tough, and they knew it, and they exulted in that knowledge.

As they approached the tree-line they heard the sounds of men rapidly approaching yelling and screaming. The air came alive with sound and movement; nothing could be seen but rolling mist. Brendan hit the tree-line with cold mist on his face. An atmosphere of tense expectations gripped him and the Marines as they waited for anticipated contact. Out of the fog rose a vast, growing sound. Peering out across the mist, they watched and listened to strange warriors screeching and yelling, stirring themselves into a shark-like feeding frenzy. Then he heard that rippling sound that raised the hair, that high thin scream from far away coming out of the mist unbodied and terrible, inhuman. It got inside him for a suspended second. It was the scream of a flood of charging men; some squat and broad, some tall and grim, with high helms and sable shields. Hundreds and hundreds more were pouring over the valley floor. The tide of humanity flowed up to the hastily drawn defensive positions of the Marines. Thunder rolled in the valley.

Brendan's radio came alive as one of his platoon leaders called him with strange reports and sightings.

"Alpha 6, this is one, over"

"One, what have you got?"

"Six, this is one, my point elements are into the wood-line and we have strange looking people coming at us screaming."

"Alpha One, protect yourself"

"Alpha 6 roger; we're moving . . . get down! Over there! Open up!"

Pop . . . Pop . . . Pop! M-16 fire could be heard over the net. Something was terribly wrong. How did the guerrilla force know they were there? Why did the terrain appear to be a different green, a different shade of green? This was not the kind of terrain he experienced just yesterday in Columbia.

Arrows thick as rain came whistling down upon the Marines, and fell clinking and glancing on the rocks. Some found a mark. The assault had begun, but there was no challenge by Marine firepower. The assailing hosts briefly halted, foiled by the silence. Ever and again the lightning tore aside the newly arrived darkness. Then the horde of attackers screamed, waving spear and sword, and shooting a cloud of arrows at any leathernecks that stood revealed. Brendan's well disciplined veterans looked out at them, a great tempest of war against the background of great fields of valley green.

Brazen trumpets sounded. The horde of predominately squat men surged forward. After a moments hesitation on they came. The lightning flashed; and blazoned upon every helm and shield the ghastly design of a skeleton's head was seen. They reached the defensive perimeter of the Marine lines. At last an answer came; fierce interlocking automatic fire from hundreds of modified M-16's, M-60's and M-79 grenade launchers. The attackers wavered broke and fled; and then charged again, broke and charged again; and each time like the incoming sea, they halted closer to the leatherneck positions. Again trumpets rang, and a press of roaring men leaped forth. They held their shields in front of them convinced they could stop the strange buzzing noises that were cutting them down like wheat.

The Mystery of the Angels

Lieutenant Nichols, platoon leader of 1st platoon, was running. He was headed for the opening in the tree-line, running full speed. He didn't think he was going to make it. His lungs were on fire, his legs seemed weighted and rubbery and he was pretty sure that his lungs were going to pop out of his chest like some alien slime creature. As he ran the cries became louder, and horns were blowing desperately. Fierce and shrill rose the yells of the grizzled attackers, and suddenly the horns ceased. He was temporarily separated from his unit due to the ensnarling mist. When he finally reoriented himself he fell into the protective vegetation with a crash and roll. He turned to one of his squad leaders Corporal O'Hare. "Try to imagine what it would be like to be all alone, separated from your unit. You can hear someone in the woods, but you don't know whether it's someone from your side or from the other. You don't know whether to hide, run, or just stand right where you are."

"I thought you were dead." O'Hare's interest was like a fever. His hands were clenched, his eyes bright, his thick arms coiled for battle.

The thunder was rumbling in the distance now. The lightning flickered still, far off among the hills in the northeast. A keen wind was blowing from the west again. The clouds were torn and drifting.

Lieutenant Roberts still grasping for air from the dash to the tree-line ordered his platoon sergeant to set up the mortars for immediate firing.

They struck at Lieutenant McMillan's platoon where it held down the right or southern half of a 150 yard line. This line was drawn west of the sea. The left or northern half was held by Lieutenant Nichol's men.

The attack was made skillfully at first. Some 50 of them slipped past forward elements and opened up a small gap between platoons. They were obviously there to feel out Marine positions. The Marines stopped shooting.

"Right fifty and fire for effect"

"Roger rounds on the way."

Gunny Smith was calling mortar fire on the target.

Within seconds the rounds exploded and gray smoke and fire belched from the impact area. It sounded to Golightly like vibrations of a giant locomotive's steel wheels with a wailing scream followed by a shuddering impact and explosion that lifted an entire section to his front, directly into the air with hot ripping shrapnel.

They struck at the strange warriors with bayonets and clubbed rifles and grenades, while Marine mortars converged in a hemming line fire between the lines, they killed them to a man.

In the interval between this thrust and the second attack, Brendan moved his headquarters section into reserve behind McMillan while Mastrion leapfrogged one of his squads forward to fill any gap this movement left. Shortly after this the crazed attackers came again. They charged openly, shouting and throwing javelins aimlessly. A score of them came charging at a machine gun held by Pfc. Keith Brookes and Pfc. William Carson.

The attackers were clearly silhouetted in the glare of gasoline fires lighted behind them by Marine mortars.

The Marines fired. They ducked down to reload and a bearded creature jumped into their hole thrusting with his pike. It dove into Carson's thigh. The attacker strained to withdraw it, and Brookes, a husky two hundred pounder, seized his M-16 by its muzzle and swung it around like a whip. The butt struck the man behind the head and brained him. His legs thumped the dirt as he fell.

"O'Hare!" Lance corporal Golightly shouted, his dark eyes like saucers as he jerked around, firing from the hip with his modified M-16. Two screaming men fell silent ten feet away. O'Hare raised his rifle and fired at another horn-rimmed creature. The man shouted something in a language foreign to O'Hare as he fell back. O'Hare tasted blood and knew he'd bitten his lip. A horn wailed. A line of warriors dressed in dark rags rushed forward to within twenty yards of the hastily drawn perimeter. The on-rushers stopped in unison and flung their spears as one then ducked down as Marines all along the line opened fire. Sheets of lead ripped into the attackers skirmish line. An M-60 machine gun opened up and seemed to fire for several minutes straight. The gasoline fires burned out and blackness engulfed the chaos.

A white prosperous grenade exploded. Hundreds of shadowy creatures emerged from the black hillside in skirmish lines, and came forward in neat rows carrying long swords and pikes. The M-60 machine gun raked back and forth, killing groups of them every sweep, but as soon as one row of skirmishers fell, another took their place.

Golightly fired and loaded as fast as his now bleeding hands could work. He rubbed his eyes and tried to focus. He felt dazed, his vision blurred with tears, but sheer terror made his bloody fingers work to reload and fire. Each shot was on target even when the flames dimmed. It was like firing point-blank into a crowd. He felt for his grenades, pulled the pin and threw. He grabbed another, pulled the pin, and threw. Screams told him he'd hit pay dirt.

Again the mortars cut off retreat for those infiltrating marauders and the Marines went about the work of destroying them.

"Get battalion on the net! We need supporting artillery fire ASAP." Brendan screamed into his RTO's (radio transmitter operator) ear.

"Yes sir!" replied Lance corporal Roger Henniger.

Henniger had volunteered for the Corps because he was in trouble with the law and needed some discipline to straighten his life out. He now was an integral part of the team although he was only nineteen, and he was considered one of the best radiomen in the company. He had the ability to memorize countless radio frequencies and call signs with ease. He had a photographic memory, and this combined with his unflappability, made him a perfect RTO.

A team whether squad or company size can't survive without the radio; that's what the skipper had told him, so that meant they couldn't survive without Henniger. *There it is*, he thought. He smiled to himself: he had the radio lingo down pat. *Lima Charlie* meant loud and clear; *Charlie Mike* meant continue the mission.

* * *

0530
first day

The Marines fired a red flare over the opening to the tree-line, illuminating a dark, bobbing mass of screaming men moving towards them with shields, helmets that bore horns, and carrying long spears or axes. The earth shook with the rush of thousands of feet hitting hard ground, along with the explosive shouting of commands, and horns blowing. They came running in scattered bands, their leaders leaping before them and waving long pikes. They howled in their native tongue.

"I can't raise battalion captain," cried Henniger.

"Keep trying," commanded Brendan.

"What do you make of this skipper? This is more than a guerilla band caught in a hammer and anvil tactic."

"I haven't a clue."

The fog thinned a little, but a pale still shown in the gray sky. The first platoon waited until the figures broke the tree-line on the left before they opened fire in a sudden, deafening roar. Automatic weapons spewing out streams of bullets and tracers tore into the densely packed mass of humanity invoking ghastly screams of pain. The mass kept coming with their spears held at waist high similar to a bayonet charge. Bodies tumbled by as the guttural snarling of men in combat was all around. A spray of bullets whittled their number but they still came forward, some of them falling, at last closing with the Marine defenders. Some of them jumped on Marines swinging axes, swords, and brandishing spears. The "jarheads" cut them down and moved to close with them in close combat.

In the face of the onslaught stood Pfc. Frank Grant of 1st platoon, manning an M-60 machine gun only a few hundred yards from the west side of the opening in the tree-line. Pfc. Grant fired hundreds of rounds into the attacking horde, before he took a javelin to the head. His peers knew him just as Grant, lean and swift like a greyhound. A man as convinced of victory as he was sure of his own death in battle. Grant had joined the Marines with his remark to his closest friend: "I'll see you some day, Mac—but not on this earth."

"Get that 60 working!" someone shouted. Pfc Acie Barbee grabbed Grant's M60, sighted it and fired. It was impossible to miss. Across the smooth gully the entire slope straight ahead looked to be moving.

Pfc Barbee never knew whether or not he heard the muffled explosions around him for his finger was squeezing the trigger of Grant's M-60 machine gun that his friend had found important enough to die for, and the charging enemy was falling back. He felt sick and dizzy as he crawled toward a stand of oak saplings and leaned against them to steady himself. They returned, again and again, sweeping in on other fronts, but the line held. The Marines fought with flamethrowers, with grenades, with bayonets. They fought yard by yard, killing and being killed, while the area they were fighting in burned from the flame throwers and the mortars. It was a scene right out of Dante's HELL.

"Lance corporal Henniger did you raise battalion yet?"

"I can't get through sir!"

Groups of Marines struggling to restore their lines blundered into groups of the grizzled attackers milling around trying to get through the barbed wire hastily strung by the Marines between the first and second attack. The shooting was wild, the grenades fell among friend as well as foe, bayonets jabbed against the sound of a strange tongue and found only air. It was a battle fought beyond the direction of either commander. Brendan's men were stunned. They stumbled as they moved lifting their legs high as though fatigue had weighted them with lead. They mumbled as they talked, licking cracked dry lips with swollen tongues. It was up to 244 men holding a line 900 yards long against thousands of dirty looking bearded men. The hills spewed forth section after section of short wild looking madmen. But now the Marines were screaming their own coarse epithets at the onrushing enemy. They were firing and the bearded ones were falling. Still they came on, the equivalent of a Marine battalion rushing Brendan's right flank held by less than 50 Marines. PFC. Huey Jones caught sight of several of the dark foreboding two legged animals. He rushed them bayoneting their leader and the others fled, he then aimed his modified M-16, put it on fully automatic and killed them. He kept firing at others who took their place until he himself was killed.

"Fire for effect!" cried Nichols into his handset, "and keep it coming 'til I say stop!"

Marine mortarmen started dropping payloads down their 'stovepipes', those harmless looking tubes that fire looping trajectories, straight up and straight down, putting their missiles down chimneys if need be and dropping them like bombs into enemy formations. Nothing kills men like mortars, and no weapon is more dreaded by foot soldiers. Alpha company had ample supplies of these dreaded killers, when these strange warriors came racing across the valley floor. Once again with, with disastrous indifference to detection, their leaders had whipped them into a wild frenzy. So the short squat figures charged and Lieutenant Roberts' mortars racked and ravaged them, while small arms fire depleted the survivors who reached the wire. But still they came. It was not really a charge but a senseless death swarming. Without any idea of how deadly these weapons were, Tuirgeis sent his best brigades into a crucible of fire and steel.

It started to thunder and lightning again, and even the howls of the crazed attackers were drowned out in the clashing of the clouds, the drumming of the rain, the drawn-toppling crash of the trees being hurled to earth by the wind, and the treetop explosions of mortar shells. The defending Marines could not fight from shallow hurriedly dug out foxholes, now full of water. They lay on the top of the ground. It became a blind battle, decided, in the end, by Marine mortars "laid in by guess and by God," and the stamina of the individual Marine.

A rain of enemy arrows came down on Gunny Smith. Arrows spattered off the ridge shale, spurting, squealing away in ricochet, Smith kept firing. Several men ran to him with more ammunition, Smith kept firing. One of them went down with an arrow in the belly. Another reached Smith, took an arrow in the groin, and went down kicking, nearly knocking Smith off balance. The other came in with an ammo box and an arrow in the shoulder. As he stopped to grab more ammo, Smith saw an arrow lodge in the third Marine's throat.

"Get the hell back!" Smitty yelled to his men as he triggered a long searing sweeping burst and the short crazed men vanished from sight like puppets pulled on a string. Then gunnery sergeant Smith charged himself. He called to his riflemen.

"Let's go!" He yelled.

Straight downhill they charged, screaming their rebel yells, firing from the hip as they went, obliterating all before them while Smith aimed a disemboweling burst at the warrior chieftain who had popped up out of the grass.

The Mystery of the Angels

It was everywhere, a cloying caking dust that was thick and clogged in the nostrils, coarse in the throat and clotted in the corner of the eyes. It swirled in dense clouds or sparkled in tiny jewels within those shafts of sunlight sometimes made visible by explosions that rent one cloud of dust only to start another.

The shooting stopped suddenly. The mortars had ended the resistance. Bodies lay torn and unrecognizable. No piece of equipment or weapon left intact. As he reached the bottom of the depression Smith heard voices. He peered from behind a bush down in the creek bed. A thin layer of mist hung over the dead like a ghostly cloud. Eight attackers were busy carrying their dead and wounded to a flat spot directly below him.

Smith put down his modified M-16 and took two grenades from his pistol belt. He pulled the pins, held down the spoons on the grenades, and slowly rose up on his knees. He tossed the grenades down the bank, grabbed his weapon, and rolled behind the bush. The grenades blew simultaneously. He jumped to his feet and ran down the bank, firing at four stunned survivors. Two jerked and were flung backwards with the impact of the bullets. The other two ran. Gunny Smith shot one of short squat men in the buttocks, spinning him around. Smith tried to shoot again, but his weapon was empty. The second warrior was hobbling away and had just reached a stream bed when Smith caught up to him and slammed his rifle butt savagely into his back. The grizzled warrior screamed in pain and fell into the water. Smith threw his arms around the man's neck, yanking up as he drove his knife down into the man's back. The warrior's neck popped with a loud crack. Smith released the lifeless body, picked up his weapon, and started to stand when an arrow whizzed by his head.

The attacker who had been shot in the buttocks had recovered enough to start firing from his long-bow. Smith stood when he saw the warrior put another arrow into his bow. The wounded enemy was fumbling with his weapon when he glanced up and saw the gunny slowly walking towards him. His eyes widened as Smith brought up his modified M-16 to his hip and fired. Smith kept his finger on the trigger and held the recoiling weapon tightly as he pumped rounds in to the slumping warrior.

Smith emptied the magazine, took another magazine from his belt and fired again, putting a bullet into the head of each man.

Brendan's right was in serious trouble. Lieutenant McMillan's platoon had been cut into small pockets among a surging sea of enemy. He was down to less than 25 effectives and he was being driven back. The horned rimmed nemesis stabbed two of McMillan's squad leaders to death and wounded one other, driving on farther to the rear after the Marine guns jammed when the crazed attackers tried to grab them and use them as clubs. During the next half hour the wild looking creatures began to falter under rising Marine firepower. They still rushed the Marines, but when they reached that point where the bullets crisscrossed with an angry steady whispering, they began to peel off in groups, flitting through the rain-washed illumination of the shell flashes to throw themselves down in the darkness and crawl toward the Marine lines on their bellies. Sometimes Gunny Smith and his men turned their pistols and rifles around to take on the infiltrators.

Marine mortar shells fell with dreadful accuracy. Death swept suddenly and invisibly among those strange looking creatures, devastating them. Regrouping they swarmed blindly up the hill against Brendan's men. They were raked with small arms. They fled back across the valley floor, sprinting in terror through that hell of mortar fire and up the side of an opposing ridge, only to re-emerge on the crest in full view of Brendan's Marines. They were riddled. Better armed attackers came surging forward. One of them a bear of a man, howled his war cry as he pushed through towards the front of the attack, knocking his companions aside with a gigantic silver shield. His sword flashed around its edge, and the whites of his fierce eyes shone over its top. So fast and powerful was his charge that he misjudged and his first swing sliced right over the gunny's head, striking another Marine. The blow sliced off the leatherneck's head as a birch switch might take the bud from a flower stalk. It dropped to the ground, eyes still blazing at the attacker. The body twitched convulsively where it fell, arms and legs striking out. Blood trickled through the cracks into the earth.

The leader of the attackers was one of those commanders who pressed home attacks that were no better than massed death-swarmings. They could not fight and run away, these commanders. They would not fight another day. They would look on death before defeat. They rushed into the massed fire of mortars, into the murderous interlocking fire of machine guns, rifles and automatic weapons. They were like moths, seeking to obliterate the light with their exploding bodies. They matched flesh against steel and were torn apart.

The strange looking attackers could not capitalize upon the first shattering charge. The assaulting troops so far from overwhelming the position, now merely flowed up against it, thrashing about in the foliage that engulfed them, tripped them, confused them, once they had left the straight going of the open valley. So now the battle was fragmented, man against man, bayonets and pikes jabbing against sounds, a mindless melee raging beyond the control of either commander.

Golightly saw the movement from the corner of his eye and began to swing his modified M-16 around, but he suddenly felt heavy. His right side felt as if it had been hit with a baseball bat. He could see the small warrior shooting his bow at him but couldn't make his body respond to bring his weapon around. His mind fought through the pain and focused on the enemy warrior. His left hand jerked the weapon around, and he fired. The bearded soldier's head snapped back and his horned helmet floated momentarily in midair before falling on his lifeless body. Golightly toppled over.

"Tonto is hit" cried O'Hare running to his fire team leader's side.

"Shit," mumbled Smith "how bad?"

O'Hare tore open Golightly's fatigue shirt and quickly assessed the damage. "He'll make it! The arrow ricocheted off his canteen and sliced his side." O'Hare then looked around and cried "Medic!" then looked at Golightly "a shot of pain killer and you're as good as new, old buddy."

The air was thick with things flying around during the battle. Spears, wood splinters, rocks. One of the apparent leaders of the attacking force was waving to one of his men when a bullet hit him in the side of the head. The blow staggered him and sent him reeling sideways. He slammed into a large tree trunk, a trunk that would have been large enough to stop a tank, much less a human.

They struck the Marine lines numerous times, falling savagely on the center and the flanks. Each time they ran into overwhelming firepower forcing them back. Betrayed by their own virtues—ardor and obedience—the short stumpy bearded warriors leaped erect and charged, coming in a swarm to be obliterated by Marine rifle fire or the hosing of the flamethrowers.

A horned rimmed attacker lowered his pike and charged O'Hare with a shoulder height thrust. O'Hare turned his back as he dropped to his left knee, going under the pike thrust. He spun on the knee with his right leg out in an "iron broom" foot sweep that took the attacker off his feet and onto his back, O'Hare struck at the man's throat as hard as he could with the knife edge of his gloved hand. Something cracked. He then jumped up and stomped him with all his might in the groin.

Maniacal voices began bellowing over the field of battle. The ground shook. Flares cast their ghostly light. Short squat men and their armament went flying through the air. The ground to the left front became a "slaughter pen". Within it the short stocky men began to run amuck. They screamed in terror. Those who survived fled back from whence they came, where the Marine mortar pursued and punished.

The several batteries of Marine mortar began firing again, machine guns swept the field and the screams of the attackers were audible to the Marines.

The corpsmen worked throughout the clamor of battle. They laid the men out on stretchers, giving plasma and morphine. Marine riflemen guarded them as they worked, for sometimes the bearded creatures from hell attempted to sneak down to the valley floor and shoot their strong bows into the casualties.

One of them appeared on the left flank brandishing a javelin. A Marine charged him and bayoneted him in the belly and then shot the bayonet free.

If the virtue of these strange warriors from hell was their tenacity, as it was, then the defect of that virtue was their inflexibility. It began to rain in torrents, and the bedraggled squat men charged Brendan's company by the hundreds, so many of them that the ground shook beneath their feet. They hit the barbed wire even as the Marine guns erupted in a bedlam of firing.

Officers of the grazed crowd were at the head of each of their respective sections, shouting and waving their swords. The attack was now veering toward the center of Brendan's line. The hordes were rushing straight into Gunny Smith's machine guns, and his gunners raked them at full trigger. The gun barrels were red and sizzling they were so heated up. But they continued to stutter on, tumbling the onrushing grizzled attackers piling them up so high that the enemy flood began to ebb and flow back across the valley floor.

Sargeant Joseph Downs was known as Jumpin' Joe, after a famous World War II Marine, for his exuberant style in the field. Like his namesake, he looked a little like a buccaneer, big and raw-boned, with a cut-down bayonet knife dangling from his cartridge belt alongside a .38 revolver stick in a special quick draw holster. Under his left armpit was a .45 shoulder holster. If it were not true that Jumpin' Joe had used these weapons, as a Recon Marine in the Gulf War and later in Somalia, the effect might have been a caricature of what is supposed to be a type of Marine sergeant. But Jumpin' Joe was genuine as he walked calmly among his men directing and adjusting their line of fire.

Pfc Fauver peered around a tree trunk and saw two of the strange creatures lying beside each other, firing arrows from cross-bows toward his left flank. He brought up his M-79 and fired. The spin-stabilized grenade landed beside the closest warrior, exploding and knocking one over onto his stunned comrade. O'Hare stepped out from behind Fauver and pumped half of a magazine into the two men, finishing them off.

A half a dozen times those strange creatures attacked the left of the Marine line, and a half a dozen times they were hurled back. The fight raged for hours and was not spent until late in the afternoon before it was over. They finally fell in a hissing volley of grenades. So tightly were they bunched, so oblivious were they to the death that swept among them, that they, at one time, overwhelmed 1st platoon and ripped a hole in the lines. The flanking Marine platoon bent back their flanks and beat back the intruders.

Joseph Murphy

1300
First day

Gunny Smith squinted. The rain had quit but the sky was still low and gray. He could see that there were ragged bodies in the valley and he went to work at once examining twenty—nine men sprawled about the battle site to his immediate front; many of the bodies mutilated by the grenades and mortar strikes. Some lay on their backs with arms extended in various distorted positions of those who suffer death suddenly and violently. Some lay on their sides, glazed eyes open, stiffened in a fetal position. Quickly he searched the bodies, gathering their swords and shields into a heap. Afterwards, he went around examining the dead ghostly sentinels, tipped his soft cover in respect, thought of his own dead, tested his body, still sound, still trustable through a long night, but weaker noticeably weaker, the heart uneven, the breath failing. But there was at least one good fight left. His mind wandered. He noted that these troops, unlike those encountered in the past several weeks wore strange leggings, they were clad in what appeared to be multiple layers of rags, faded colors of berry-dye fabric peeking out through rents in shapeless garments that might have once been women smocks. In addition, they were covered with animal fur and helmets with horns. There were no weapons other than spears, strong bows, and battle axes. He picked out from the pile of grim weapons several knives, and searching further he found black sheaths. He grasped an arrow by the shaft, twisted it carefully out of the dirt. It was fletched with the split tail-feathers of a woodpecker, he saw, and banded with the blue thread, wrapped in a line half an inch wide below the quills.

"This gear is strange to me."

If he didn't know better these bodies resembled warriors, from another time frame; called *Genti,* a term the Irish used to describe the *heathens or Vikings.* It seemed inconceivable, but all appearances pointed to him being someplace where the customs, dress and weaponry still held sway. He would have thought the whole thing a fantasy of sorts, had it not been for the dead and wounded on both sides. The behavior of the attacking force and the weaponry they possessed existed nowhere but in Ireland; in a time gone by. In addition, the accents of the people in battle left no doubt of that. He shook irritably, hugging his elbows against the slight chill air. He couldn't admit for a moment the completely implausible idea that he was in another time frame than his own. Columbia, after all had stood in its present location for centuries. It was there; but the hard evidence before him confounded him.

Marine and attackers were in some cases intertwined and as Smith bent down, he found Grant; he then began to scratch the black dirt into his fingers. Smith lowered his head again to hide the emotions that flooded him. Slowly very slowly words began to flow. No one in front of him was moving. His voice broke, and his eyes suddenly moistened. He said softly, "We all have value; we're worth something more than the dirt. I never saw dirt that I'd die for, what we're all fighting for, in the end, is each other. We are a band of brothers." There was love and mutual admiration between Frank Grant and the gunny, and no abler combination has ever been arrayed for battle. Grant had fought through a lot of engagements in the gulf war, his battle skirmishes numbered twenty, and he was accustomed to attacking at every opportunity. Smith looked around, searching. He wanted a place to be alone. The barbed—wire perimeter fence was off to his right. He headed quickly for its solitude. He'd prepared himself a long time ago. It was part of his job. He knew friends would die. It was the price one had to pay for membership in an outfit that dealt in death. He smiled through the hurt. Smitty stopped and took a deep breath. He would return in a few minutes. He would put the thoughts of his friend in a special place. He wouldn't carry his remorse. It affected thoughts, actions, and decisions. It would eat away at a man's mind. He was a man in charge, enlisted wise, of a Marine Infantry Company. He wasn't allowed the luxury of remorse. His mind had to be clear with no distractions. His life, his Company, depended upon it. Smitty raised his head and looked skyward as tears streamed down his face.

Please, Lord, take care of him. There has to be a heaven, Lord, there's just got to be a place where he can fulfill his dreams. Please, Lord, take care of him and the others . . . make them happy.

The mist had given the whole affair an air of eerie authenticity so effective that even O'Hare who not only knew that he was in Columbia less than twenty-four hours ago, could almost believe he was watching the real thing. He refused to believe this was real. He shouted to no one in particular, and then covered his face with his hands.

"This is a nightmare!" he cried "A nightmare with no end! God, please let me wake up!"

O'Hare's heart was hammering as if it would burst. He put the flat of his hand against the sound and made himself relax. Closing his eyes, he practiced a mental relaxation technique, focusing his skills on himself as he cradled his weapon waiting for the next assault.

Out of the dust, just before dark, limped the dirtiest Marine Gunny Smith had seen so far. A quarter-inch of grime coated his beardless face while a lock of blond hair hung from beneath his helmet. The youth's name was Alfred Clark and he broke the silence by saying "Somebody give me a pack of cigarettes; there's a machine gun crew out there in a shell hole and there ain't one of 'ems got a butt."

Smitty grinned and the silence was broken.

* * *

As the corpsmen worked on, they loaded the wounded aboard the stretchers. Others took the casualties to the rear of the front lines. But there were no lines as such; there were groups of Marines who had dug in here or fortified an abandoned foxhole there. There were gaps everywhere. Flanks were dangling. The advance toward the tree-line could be measured in hundreds of yards, others in scores of feet. Some troops were still trapped in the open. By then it was early evening, and the Marines halted and dug in, as drenching rains broke over their heads. The sound of rolling drums beat faster; then it was over the forest and the valley floor and the water was swishing, streaming, and gurgling earthward. It was as nothing these Marines had seen before. It was not a rain storm; a spell of rain, it was hours of it. It was the cloudburst in perpetuity, and it was so constant.

A bitter aching fatigue had come upon them. They had met the enemy in the valley, in the wood-line and atop the ridge; they had defeated him. They had been battered by every weapon these wild-ass creatures could throw at them. They had not slept. They had been ravaged by the rains, weakened by dysentery, nagged by ulcers and had developed foot rot. They had met each ordeal with the hope of victory and survived only to prepare for greater trial.

The attack which had begun in early hours of the morning was over by late afternoon that same day. The descending sun revealed a hideous spectacle on that field of battle. Nothing moved.

* * *

1700
First day

All through the night, cries of "Corpsman!" "Corpsman!" were raised. Men wounded during the day, men who fought on while wounded, were dying from loss of blood. And there was a shortage of blood plasma, of bandages.

"Doc" Ronald Sinclair had patched up two dozen or so men left of the 40 whom lieutenant Mastrion had led against the central sector. Sergeant Amato Anthony had been shot in the head. Sinclair had fixed up the lieutenant's leg with splints and bandaged the sergeant's head.

In the afternoon as more wounded were brought back to medic station, Doc Sinclair was forced to take medical kits from the bodies of fallen corpsmen. He even stripped dead Marines of what medical supplies they were carrying.

The corpsmen worked through the darkness in a "makeshift hospital." The position had been vacated by the Marines and the corpsmen had set up an operating room inside, and worked on the wounded with the aid of flashlights.

"We're out of anesthetics," one of the corpsmen whispered. Another one shrugged. There were things he had to cut and things he had to sew, and they had to be done, with or without the pain.

They worked on. There were sometimes moans, occasionally an uncontrollable sob, but mostly there was silence while the flashlight beams played on hands and bullets continued to echo in the distance.

Joseph Murphy

The stress of battle brought the sweat oozing from the bodies staining and making blotches on the pale green camouflaged fatigues of the Marines. There was tension in the air. Marines squatted, blacking rifle sights or applying a last light coat of oil to their rifle bores. Machine gunners went over long belts of ammunition coiled wickedly in oblong green boxes, carefully withdrawing and reinserting the cartridges into their cloth loops, making certain that they would not stick and jam the guns. Other men inspected grenade pins or camouflage nets for their helmets. They were ready.

* * *

Recon Patrol

Brendan needed to know what he ran into and what was in front of him. Thus, his decision to send out a night recon patrol was to find out what was going on. Patrols were the eyes and ears of a line of defense, the feelers went out probing for the presence of the enemy. They went out in squad strength. They were lightly armed men. The men only carried a canteen of water. They fastened their gear tight to prevent tell-tale clinks, they daubed their faces with cami-stick, adorned their blouses and helmets with branches; and moved slowly, hugging the trails to the right and left with intervals of a dozen feet between them, listening for the sudden cry of birds that might betray a lurking enemy, sometimes moving at a crawling, crablike rhythm, at a pace so maddeningly slow that tension became multiplied, all the sounds so magnified that the rustling of a small animal might echo in helmet muffled ears like the movement of a human body.

With that the recon patrol plunged into the darkness. O'Hare left the tracking to Golightly, whose wound was now heavily bandaged. There was little for him to see. The floor of the forest was dry and covered with a drift of leaves; but guessing that the enemy would stay near water, he returned often to the banks of the stream.

Dusk deepened. Mist lay behind them among the trees below and brooded on the pale margins valley, but the sky was clear for now. Stars came out. The waxing moon was riding in the west and the shadows of the rocks were black. The moonlight made walking deceptive; though they could see every detail of the ground, they had no depth perception; flat plants and jagged stones looked the same height, causing them to lift their feet absurdly high over nonexistent obstacles and stub their toes on protruding rocks. They walked as fast as they could, listening for the sounds of the night. The dark bulk of a mountain rose to the east, while far below to the south the foothills ran out into a vast barren moorland. The top of the rocks sloped inwards from all sides, forming a shallow dish. In the center of the dish was a blackened circle, with the sooty remnants of charred sticks. They were not the first visitors there.

The dale ran like a stony trough between the ridged hills, and a trickling stream flowed among the boulders at the bottom. A cliff frowned upon their right; to their left rose gray slopes, dim and shadowy in the late night. They walked three more hours, down into darkness. Rain started up again, a steady drizzle that soaked them through and made it impossible to keep dry. They moved warily concerned about possible ambushes. They continued to climb, past the spot where the rude path petered out into clumps of gorse and heather. They were among foothills there, and the granite rocks rose higher than O'Hare's head. There in the cool wet hour before dawn they rested for a brief space. The moon had long gone down before them, the stars glittered above them; the first light of day had not yet come over the dark hills behind them.

* * *

O'Hare awoke to a gentle tap. Golightly was kneeling next to him, putting on his ruck. O'Hare slipped his arms through the lightened pack and rose slowly. Within minutes they were walking next to the trail and river. They moved for fifteen minutes, when Golightly stopped and snapped his fingers lightly. O'Hare starred at Golightly who was slowly lowering himself to a kneeling position on the ground and motioning the corporal to come close to him.

The recon patrol saw what they at first took to be boulders, lying at the foot of the slope, instead they were huddled bodies. Five dead people lay there. They had been hewn with many cruel strokes, and two had been beheaded. The ground was wet with their dark blood.

"In the wrong place, at the wrong time;" whispered a member of the patrol.

Both men were soaked with sweat. Walking with such concentration drained a man quickly, but their senses had been fine-tuned, and they'd learn the trail. They now knew its natural sounds, the creaks of the old trees and the swishing of the tall grass. Every nerve ending tingled. It was a sensation most men would never feel. It was like fear but not fear, like elation but not joy, a high without a stimulus. It was like a hunter that could attack unseen and unheard. They walked a tightrope on which their balance was instinct and senses. If either failed, they would fall to certain destruction.

* * *

Cut off from battalion, Brendan and his men passed an anxious but uneventful remainder of the night, and in the morning, while the mists began to shred over the forest roof, Brendan was glad he had sent out patrols.

* * *

They were among hills again, and traveling on a track wider than any they had seen for the past several hours. Not only that, but it showed signs of recent use-heavy use-so much, in fact the patrol moved off the main road into the forest. The walking was much more difficult there. Wide-eyed in the bushes, the patrol knew for the first time what it meant to be paralyzed by terror. They spotted Genti on horse, their armor clanked as they rode. Leather tunics wrinkled like heavy skin, and capes swelled behind like bats' wings. Helmets slung from their saddles grinned like monstrous skulls. Most hideous were their weapons. Quivers of iron-tipped arrows rattled on their backs, and great bows of horn and sinew curved across their shoulders. Maces and spiked chains swung from their saddles. All carried swords hooked at the end, for gutting; apparently hot on the scent of some unfortunate devils whose path had crossed their own.

"Take the point, Tonto," O'Hare called to Golightly as he stopped to fix something on his pack.

Swiftly now the patrol turned and followed the path that contained many footprints; and with adrenalin pumping they sprang from stone to stone. Golightly, the point man of that patrol was a twenty-first century gladiator, a man who fought a war at its most personal level. And like the gladiator he could lose the game but once. If the pilot of a drone was on one end of a war's spectrum, the point man was at the other end. Tonto, as he loved to be called, was filled with the sense of power he always felt while walking point; the power of knowing he held death in his hands and would be the first to use it. He loved that feeling. He was considered a '*somebody*' when he walked point. He was the man he always wanted to be—respected, tough, and indispensable. At last they reached the crest of the gray hill, and a sudden breeze blew in their face and stirred their damp uniforms, the chill wind of dawn. Golightly slowed as he saw the smoke drifting upwards.

It looked clear, just mountains and valleys of undisturbed green. He led the patrol downhill about twenty yards, then along the slope, trying to parallel the direction of the proposed march. The terrain leveled out slightly where two mountain masses joined. Golightly glanced back to make sure the others were keeping up. He moved cautiously, feeling cold chills run up his back. Before him the gritty mist was dissipating and revealed the broken, shattered earth. He stopped as his stomach knotted uncontrollably. He could smell and feel the unmistakable aura of death.

*   *   *

0445
Village of Rawa
Second day

Turning back the recon patrol saw day leap into the sky across the far hills. The red rim of the sun rose over the shoulders of the dark land. Before them in the northwest the world lay still, formless and green; but even as they looked the shadows of night melted, the colors of the waking earth returned.

They now tracked their evasive foe by the clear light of day. It seemed that the aggressors, for some strange reason, had pressed on with all possible speed. Every now and then the pursuers found things that had been dropped or cast away. The patrol went in single file like hounds on a strong scent, and an eager light was in their eyes. Nearly due west a broad swath of trampled grass was bruised and blackened. These were the tale-tale signs of the enemy force as they continued on.

They pressed on until they reached a causeway across a vast and steamy peat bog. Creatures from another age bellowed in the distance, their howls swirling in the mists so that they seemed to loom over them. Twice, when leathery birds swept past on creaking wings the patrol ducked for cover. Past the marsh, the road wound through a range of flat-topped hills and at last reached a broad plateau. Here in the morning of the following day, they came to a crossroad; a place of death.

The smoke, they spotted earlier, rose to their immediate front. Signs pointed to a huge battle having been fought in the surrounding area. Many men had died. So steeped was the place in horror that the patrol could feel it, even while they stood on the last slope looking down. They could feel the charge and the clash of cavalry. They could hear the terrible song of arrow volleys, the hiss and smack of swords on leather armor, and the shrieks of slaughtered horses and mangled men. They could hear merciless laughter and screams as captive throats were slashed and torturers set to their grisly work. They could smell blood, and flayed flesh, and the stench of burning meat. Even from where they stood they could see the mounded graves, the scattered bones.

"Water can't be too far ahead. I hear rushing water." Golightly whispered

They heard it before they saw it. It was further on over a jumble of stone and through a crevice, into the head of a tiny glen, rock-walled and leafy. It was filled with the gurgling of water from the burn that spilled from a dozen small falls among the rocks and plunged roistering down the length of the defile into a series of rills and pools below. The rushing water fell fifteen feet before crashing onto huge glistening boulders that smoked with a thin cloud of mist. Miniature rainbows appeared in the wet cloud. Swallows dipped low over the water to drink, and plovers and woodcocks poked long bills into the muddy earth at its edges, digging for insects. Golightly stopped near the pool and dropped to one knee. It had been a tough hour of moving since their last break. His fatigues were soaked with sweat. He motioned to O'Hare to come forward. Golightly's camouflaged-painted face was streaked. O'Hare knelt beside him. He didn't have to whisper; the crashing water made it difficult even to talk normally. "We'll take fifteen and give everybody a chance to catch their breath.

A few members of the patrol clambered on to a great tree-root that wound down into the stream, and stooping drew up some water in their cupped hands. The water refreshed them and seemed to cheer their hearts; for a while some of the patrol wadded into the stream, cooling their sore feet and legs.

* * *

O'Hare stood from where he had been filling his canteen and carefully moved around the pool looking for telltale signs. The M-79 seemed ridiculously small for him. He held it in one hand easily. The M-79 was a small but lethal single-shot, breech-loading weapon that fired 40mm spin-stabilized grenades with a bursting radius of about five meters. The launcher also fired other types of rounds: high explosive, smoke, signal, gas, and buckshot. No sign of anything. The stream broadened and became slow moving and tranquil on its meandering trek to the river. Only a few tenacious rays of light penetrated the cloud cover above, and the small gold spots they made on the earth seemed to smoke as notes of dust rose upward and were softly illuminated. The dank smell of damp rotting organic life was pungent and seemed heavy in their lungs. A pair of iridescent butterflies fluttered in front of him as he waded carefully through the pebble-strewn stream. The sudden absence of sound was unnerving. They had become used to the gurgling, laughing water that rushed over the rocks from pool to pool.

It was quiet. Uneasy, the patrol moved cautiously, trying to peer through the dazzling clouds of mist. Golightly thought of home and how morning was the nosiest time of the day. Fish jumped in the lake, dogs barked, cattle moaned to be milked and fed, and myriad birds greeted the dawn from high perches. But here there was no sound, except the distant rumble of the river and the crackling sound of fire. No children shouted from the village, as they approached, no animals announced their presence.

On the other side of the moorland was a stretch of twisted rocks, pitted and gouged by the advance and retreat of glaciers long gone. Rainwater filled the deeper pits. And thistle and tansy and meadowsweet surrounded these tarns with thick growth, the flowers, reflected in the still water. They were in sloping foothills, now, thick with heather. Just beyond, the countryside changed abruptly, surrounded by clusters of sycamore and larch. They came over the crest of the hill, and left the plovers crying by the tarns behind them.

Sterile and fishless, these pools dotted the landscape and formed traps for the unwary, who might easily stumble into one.

Before entering the village, O'Hare and Henniger, the RTO stripped down to just their weapons, and moved across the open field facing the village and vanished into the mist like animals, soundlessly, crouched low. Henniger whispered into his radio handset to the remainder of the patrol left behind.

"Recon I this is lone wolf. How do you hear me? Over"

"This is Recon I, we have you *Lima Charlie;* Over"

"This is lone wolf. I got you same same. Out"

Recon I didn't wait too long. In a few minutes lone wolf was back.

"It appears deserted; however, there is death all over the place," he reported.

"Every last house; plates are still on the table, and weapons on the wall." He led them into the center of the village.

The sun was rising, reflecting off low clouds, and the afterglow drenched the place in red. Close up, it was even more horrible than it had been from the hilltop. The contorted remains of horses and men lay everywhere some mere skeletons, some dried black, some fresh and putrefying.

Death and destruction abounded. Men, women, and children were butchered; the village smoldering.

* * *

The Marines moved cautiously through the village to discover there were still some living beings.

The village was a shambles. It was a poor village; far poorer than anything they had seen so far. The houses were small, the barns dilapidated. The Marine recon patrol moving through the place was leery of every sound in that awful hellhole; the creaking of shutters banging in the wind, the grumbling of enormous frogs in the bog beyond the crossroads, the howling of wolves or dogs far away. Except for a few ambulatory people left, nothing lived in that place. The horrible remnants of the battle lay where they had fallen. Corpses sprawled everywhere, people slaughtered even as they were stripping off their leather aprons and reaching for their swords. The bodies of the women and children hunched where they had been dropped. Those remaining uttered plaintive cries as they drifted above the carnage. But in spite of the surprise the villagers had acquitted themselves well, for there were many Genti corpses too, their gruesome fingers splayed, their faces frozen forever in grimaces of death.

The few people left were hurrying about, avoiding the corpses that lied everywhere; as they gathered in a meeting hall. This was the largest and oldest building in the village, what was left of it. The landscape was the bleakest and most awful any Marine had ever seen. Great fires must have raged there, leaving charred rock and cadaverous forests. No flowers grew; no birds sang. Noises echoed down the valley distorted and magnified like the groans of Earth itself.

All light bantering ceased. The patrol turned aggressive and savage. Marines hoped openly for battle, and because they had also not yet known it, talked loudly of wanting the enemy to come because they wanted to kill him and chop him up with his own swords and pikes.

Joseph Murphy

* * *

0530
Company HQ
Second day

Brendan called his platoon leaders together; he spoke quickly and bluntly bringing them up to date on what Recon I reported. They were completely alone and God only knew if or when they would receive support from Regiment.

* * *

The recon patrol moved on, and as the Marines continued to patrol the outskirts of the village, the point man of the patrol froze and the rest of the patrol followed suit. Silhouetted against the sunrise on the opposite ridge line was a troop of mounted men, the gleam of metal on both the horses and riders suggesting they had a military nature. The horsemen after hovering for a moment came down the hill approaching slowly.

CHAPTER FIVE

Treating the wounded

Remember that death is lighter than a feather,
But that Duty is heavier than a Mountain
—Motto of the Sendai Division
Re-script of Emperor Meiji

0600
Outskirts of Rawa
Second day

Suddenly the valley came alive. With a surging cry members of the recon patrol threw off their coverings and lunged up out of shallow pits where they were laying. So fast were they, and so complete was the surprise that before Alfrey and Iarnkne could do anything the first of the recon patrol were upon them.

Muirgel saw them emerge; huge men with green faces. She shut her eyes then opened them quickly. They were still there. She tried to raise her head. Pain raced through her body, making her shudder and moan uncontrollably. Her eyes squinted as she gritted her teeth. She forced her eyes back open and watched the giant men.

Alfrey, Iarnkne and Muirgel were taken back when the strange men appeared out of nowhere with even stranger sticks pointing at them. No matter how skilled the knights were they were completely outnumbered and surrounded by these odd looking warriors.

"Stand back. My lady is injured" screamed Iarnkne as he instinctively drew his sword.

* * *

0615
Company HQ
Second day

"Alpha six, this is Recon one, over."
"Recon one, this is Alpha six, read you loud and clear."
"Six, we have picked up several friendlies, one is wounded."
"Recon one, stay where you are and tend to the wounded, we will see you in three."
"Roger that six."

* * *

0730
Village of Rawa
Second day

Inside, it smelled of wood smoke and fleece, and although cool from the draft, was warmer then Brendan expected without a working fire. The only source of light was the doorway and a small window as they allowed the gray day to pour into the hut. Framed in that watery light, Muirgel huddled across the chamber from the doorway. Furs were pulled tightly around her. The wall she leaned against lacked the whitewash and mud plaster applied to its exterior.

The only sound was the patter of rain on the window's shutter and the hiss and pop of the coals in the brazier's brass pan beneath it. Curled in furs, her splendid red hair tumbling free, she looked innocently beautiful. Even if one had not been bedazzled by magical fairy dust, it would have been hard to believe that she was so young. It would have been hard to imagine her dead. She radiated life; glowing, pure, and exuberant. She was eighteen, handsome with the aloof confidence of a woman who lived out-of-doors. Her arms and face, and the V at her throat where her garment opened, were slightly tanned. She did not freckle in the sun, despite her pale skin and her red hair. The brazier, a flat copper pan lifted on a tripod, gleamed as ruddy as the coals within it.

She turned restlessly in her straw bed. She shoved the blanket away and felt the cool breeze from the rain touch her lightly. She put aside the linen, letting the moving air caress her body. She dreamed of peaceful pursuits. She was restless and breathing heavily from her exertions. Her body was covered with perspiration which had soaked her short garment, causing it to cling to her in the most revealing ways. A strong '*fall*' smell emanated from her body.

"If you dress that way, woman you might just as well be wearing nothing at all." Brendan prudishly told himself.

He crouched before the hearthstone and brought out his zippo lighter which performed the miracle of bringing forth life-giving warmth from dead wood. Moments later, knife-edged shadows danced against the hut's walls. Smoke curled its way up to the blackened spot in the thatch. Newborn heat reached out to envelop him.

Brendan froze where he stood. The fire's golden light gleamed against her damp skin and her hair was silhouetted against the fires glow. It didn't detract from her beauty.

Muirgel woke up coughing. Her body was in a cold sweat, in spite of the slight breeze, due to the stuffy air of the tiny thatch hut in which she had been taken. She choked back the sound, as if fearing to wake others. Lying perfectly still, she tried to sort out the terrors of the dream from the terrors of the waking world. Despite the dampness, sweat continued to pour from her body. She was afraid to sleep because her dreams were so terrible. Yet if she did not sleep, the next day would be even worse. She had barely been able to move at the end of yesterday. Would she be able to get up when the pale light of day appeared? The terror of yesterday, the strange looking inhabitants who helped her, her wound from yesterday; horrors everywhere; she rolled over restlessly on the straw bed.

As if she felt someone's attention on her, she opened her eyes. Their gazes met and held. Muirgel loosed a startled breath as something stirred within her. He made sure the front door was ajar because life and health demanded it. Just as the fire needed a draft to breathe, those inside craved the draft to carry the smoke from the interior so they didn't choke.

Brendan thought the woman's recuperative powers were astonishing. She was wounded and battered from the viscous attack; but after a few hours of tender loving care by the Marine medics she appeared to have her energy and enthusiasm back. She and Brendan were alone in the darkened thatched roof house. The brief shower that was beating loudly on the thatched roof had stopped. She was conscious of the smell of the smoldering embers in the fireplace, the smell of the outdoors wafting from Brendan, the fresh smell of the stopped rains, and wet woolen garments. She cowered back against the rough wooden wall, head down feeling that she was naked before this strange invader. He, on the other hand, was grinning at her like a pleased little boy.

"I am glad to see that you are feeling better. We had a close scare and thought we lost you, in which case that would have been a terrible tragedy. Does it hurt?"

"Yes"

"We must care for the wound before it becomes worse than it already is."

"Worse than it already is?"

"Yes, that is, I mean, inflamed, you know, with pus and swelling and fever."

"Oh, yes, I know what you mean. But do you mean to say you know what to do for that? Are you a charmer?"

"No not me, but I have men with me who are called medics and they know how to deal with that."

He approached her to examine the wound. They were close enough that he could smell the scent of flowers from her skin. Her eyes narrowed. Sensing her concern, "If I were a bad guy I would have carried you away on sight. But I am only a Marine company commander trying to figure out what the hell is going on and you are safer with me in this house than if there were a bevy of nuns here."

He thought of opening the shutters on the tiny window to let in the sunlight that was trying to break through the clouds but decided against it. The gloom of the candle flame fit his dark mood more than the implacable August sun.

"I can see you are the leader of these—eh—strange men. Are you a King?" Muirgel asked softly.

"I am the leader of these men but I am not a King. Who are you and what is your name?"

"My name is Muirgel, daughter of King Maelsechlainn (Mal-sec-lane) of Meath"

"Meath, as in Ireland?"

"Yes"

"What the hell is going on? What are we doing here? This must be a bad dream."

Just then a woman of the village, knowledgeable in herbs, entered "Now, child, rinse your mouth with this. It will cleanse the cuts and ease the pain. Willow-bark tea," she explained in an aside to Brendan, with a bit of ground orrisroot." Brendan nodded, in agreement recalling from his botany classes that willow bark in fact contained salicylic acid, the active ingredient in aspirin.

"Wouldn't the willow bark increase the chance of bleeding?" Brendan asked. The woman nodded approvingly.

"Aye, it does sometimes. That's why you follow it with a good handful of St. John's wort soaked in vinegar. That stops bleeding, if it's gathered under a full moon and ground up well." Muirgel obediently swilled her mouth with the astringent solution, her eyes watering at the sting of the aromatic vinegar.

The woman then busied herself in preparing for the washing of Muirgel's wound. She laid out a large linen cloth in front of her, placing on it three copper basins filled with water. She proceeded to take two heated stones from the hearth and put each in a basin to warm the water. She then sat on the floor in front of Muirgel.

Coals again glowed in the brazier's pan, but that didn't stop Muirgel's breath from clouding in the air before her, even though

Brendan had successfully started a fire. With the wind thrusting icy fingers through the cracks in the shutters, the draft was so bad now that little heat stayed and the stuffiness started to dissipate. Dozens of candles stood around the room. Although their flames fluttered and danced, the light was strong enough to force the shadows into soft piles in the corners.

Muirgel had green eyes, sun bleached red hair; she was indeed very pretty. Brendan felt something stir within him. He had not been with a woman in a long time. Every movement of her subtle body was an invitation. Brendan felt a thump, a flutter in his chest. It was as if the heart was turning over. He put his hand there and passed one small breathless moment.

Outside the sun was beginning to beat against the wooden roof of the hut. The turf of Tara would be wet and muddy once again.

* * *

It would take the better part of two days for the word to spread and people to emerge from hiding and for the Marines to organize the villagers, to distribute food and give medical treatment to those that were still alive. Seeing the medics attend the wounded, feeling flesh and bone beneath their fingers, taking pulses, inspecting tongues and eyeballs, all the familiar routine, had done much to settle the feeling of hollow panic that had been with the Marines since the strange mist engulfed them. However strange their circumstances, and however out of place they might be, it was somehow very comforting to realize that there were truly other people; warm-fleshed and hairy, with hearts that could be felt beating and lungs that breathed audibly. Bad—smelling, louse—ridden, and filthy, some of them, but that was nothing new to the medics. It would be a tense two days. No one could forget the ferocity of the Genti attack. The memory was too vivid, the graves too fresh, for anyone to feel secure. O'Hare had his men continue to patrol the perimeters of the village until the time came to leave.

The sun climbed to the noon and then rode slowly down the sky. The road past the main gate to the village led up and over a small hill. Light clouds came up out of the sea in the distant south and were blown away upon the breeze. The sun sank. Shadows rose behind and reached out long arms from the east.

* * *

0540
Village of Rawa
Third day

By dawn on the third day, all was ready. They gathered, as the mist was rising, at the burial ground of the old settlement. The few remaining women wrung their hands and wept inconsolably, knowing they would be leaving this hell-hole and the loved ones they left behind.

Up and about, Muirgel was feeling stronger.

"Does Muirgel believe in fairy lands and fairy princesses?" asked Brendan.

"Maybe" she then proceeded to describe to him all the wonderful mystical things that go on in her land. All the while her feelings stirred.

She spoke to Brendan about leprechauns and legends, wonderful tales about the banshees being tricked or bribed to go away, and then, when she'd been older, true tales of the fight for freedom against the Vikings. She was keen and wise and had seen the battlefield of her Country torn to sheds, yet had somehow maintained a love for all humanity around her.

* * *

Iarnkne's lieutenant, Alfrey, offered his hand to some of the people, speaking in Gaelic their native tongue. Perhaps it was what Alfrey said, or perhaps it was that recognition. Whatever it was, the women accepted the soldier's hand, letting him pull them to their feet.

The dead had been buried, and the sally ports and main gates of Rawa had been sealed. Iarnkne and his beloved Muirgel, along with Brendan's men, moved northwest, toward Meath.

CHAPTER SIX

Lost Contact

> Corpses drifting swollen in the sea depths
> Corpses rotting in the mountain grass-
> We shall die, we shall die for our Emperor.
> We shall never look back.
> —Ancient battle oath, Umi Ukaba

Regimental HQ
Rain Forest
Northeastern Columbia

"Alpha six this is Papa Bear do you read?" The exasperated regimental RTO turned to his Commander.

"No answer sir; but I did hear what sounded like gunfire before in the background." The colonel paced back and forth before looking at the map again.

"Have we sent up any micro-mechanical drones to find out what is going on?"

"Yes sir, we have but to no avail. There seems to be a dense strange mist over the area in question."

"They may have run into an ambush themselves. Get me Delta Company. I'm going to commit my reserve."

Colonel Hull was an imposing man. He was big and broad-shouldered, with light brown hair and fierce blue eyes set in a fighting face. He was a man of quiet confidence who gave the impression of great strength, both moral and physical. He was one of those men from class and wealth who chose the military as his calling. To such officers the civilian world, the outside, was a repugnant place filled with cunning, brash, pushy, ruthless, selfish and ambitious men, while the military, "the inside," was an eminently satisfying sanctuary in which one encountered other high-principled men embodied with the same qualities of modesty, manners, morality, chivalry, courage and a sense of duty.

* * *

Isolated

"What am I doing here?" Brendan asked himself for the hundredth time. "Here in this strange place, unreachable from everything familiar, from home and friends, adrift and alone among what amounted to savages?" After the initial shock wore off, he had begun to feel strangely secure and even intermittently comfortable during the last twenty four hours; but now he realized that the comfort was likely an illusion, even if the security was not. Brendan, like his father, was a history buff and vaguely remembered a major battle in Irish history that concerned the Vikings and the Irish in and around the year 800 and something. Brendan himself was concerned about the fact that if he indeed was in the year 800 plus where was his regimental commander? "What would he do when he failed to locate one of his infantry companies? Would Brendan ever see him again?"

The feeling of "isolation" spread among the Marines. There seemed no way out, around or through. This was like a bad toothache, which can never be understood but only felt. It was a long shuddering sigh of weariness with which men rehearsed in their minds what had gone before, wondering dully, not that it had been sustained, but in what hideous shape it would reappear. It was a sense of utter loneliness made poignant by their longing for some sign of help from their regiment, which did not seem to be forthcoming. It seemed to these men that some supernatural being set them down in another time zone in the midst of an enemy they did not know and left them there to go it alone. They could not understand, had no wish to understand, why this was happening. They reasoned only as they fought that they were alone.

So they turned in upon themselves. They developed that vacant, thousand—yard stare-lusterless unblinking eyes gazing out of sunken red-rimmed sockets. They drew in upon themselves for strength. It was them against the world; and it was up to Brendan and his leadership to keep them from becoming unglued.

CHAPTER SEVEN

Encounter

Conquest, Famine, War, Death,
  —The four Horsemen of the Apocalypse

0950
Third day

Murphy's three rifle platoons pivoted to the north, while Nichols' weapons platoon advanced northeastward along the east bank of the Irish Sea behind and slightly to the rear of third platoon. The unit on the far right, third platoon, led by Lieutenant McMillan, encountered the first sizable resistance northwest of the village of Rawa; the village that had been torched by these strange men. The Genti or Viking force reacted to the encounter with the 'customary head-long assault' much like a World War II Japanese 'Banzai' charge; which was cut down by the Marines.

Moving quickly to encircle the new threat, the company commander, leading forward elements of his second platoon, came upon a clearing filled with several bearded dirty men screaming and attacking a young girl. They had pinned her to the ground; her gray dress ripped open. She struggled as they pressed her to the ground and tried to pull up her shirts. They slapped her hard across her face, ordering her to be still. Their filthy fingers were digging into her thighs wrenching them apart. They were bending over her, fondling and tormenting her. These berserk Vikings, northern devils, had burst from their dragon-ships into the mists of the ancient Irish coast, to kill and plunder and burn. These were men who would kill with the last ounce of their strength. Who would use that last strength to rape and sow their violent seed in the bellies of the conquered. They had ignored all rules of engagement in their frenzy and turned their attention to raping. Brendan charged blindly into the body of men his M-16 on fully automatic. They went down like wheat. As he reached the hysterical female more filthy screaming creatures, from an era-gone-by, came at him. His rifle jammed but the attacking madmen were cut down by the withering fire from men of his trailing second platoon.

Brendan knelt beside her, pulling her out from under the corpses. She was shaking with nerves and shock, and she clung to her unknown savior without speaking for minutes. Her eyes were blue and perfectly set. They were so angry. Her thin nose was slightly upturned, and her long thin neck was elegantly chiseled. Still without speaking he picked her up; in the din of battle, remaining still he looked around, and carried her away. He didn't seem to notice her weight. They said little to one another, conserving their energy for the task of slogging through the enveloping wetness. She, on the other hand, sobbing slightly, as her fingers splayed across the edge of his armored vest jacket, thought that although this strange man appeared slim, he was built like a rock; a lean machine, of pure, supple muscle. He turned to avoid a dead horse, still not seeming to notice that he was carrying her. The crown of her head barely touching his cheekbone she looked up into his face. Ignoring her movements, he carried her to an improvised aid station where his dead and wounded were now gathered. He gently put her down on the ground beside a thatched roof house, one of the few still standing on the outskirts of Rawa, for his medics to look after her. She tried to move and couldn't. She ached in every joint and muscle. She felt a chilly isolation, as though the autumn wind blew through her bones. Her head throbbed as he she'd been hammered with hardwood mallets. A small sound escaped her, while her head was bowed, but her shoulders were set in a harsh line and her profile could have been chiseled from granite.

Her clothes had been ripped and torn; loosened by the struggle with the rapists. Tantalizing wisps of golden blonde hair now escaped her plait. They clung to the curve of her cheeks and trailed in seductive promise along the slender length of her neck. She was beautiful, medium height, with blonde hair a far softer shade then deep gold. She had blue eyes and a face of sheer light and beauty. Her ears, nose, and mouth had been created with a stunning sense of proportion. As she lay on the ground she felt Brendan's presence so close to her. Tall, straight, striking in his camouflaged fatigues, face somewhat taut, eyes enigmatic as he trained them out into the distance on the scenery they just traversed. She saw his hand as it lay on the strange weapon he held. He had powerful hands. She was tempted, at first, to reach out and touch it. She bit her lip. His shoulders appeared broad in the strange clothing he was wearing. He had an exceptional build, lean, wiry, not an ounce of fat on his frame. He possessed a very strong jaw-line and striking features. Her shoulders trembled; she was tiring rapidly as a Marine medic drew a heavy black mantle around her pale gray dress. She had no more strength than rainwater in a barrel. He lowered his lips to her concealed ear trying to whisper something to her. She drew back another shuddering breath. There was nothing of revulsion in the sound, only deep stirring. She was near collapse, when she finally touched Brendan's hand, and Brendan felt his face getting warm in a way that had nothing to do with the heat from the fires and adrenalin pumping through him from the battle. He would try to tell her that he was glad she was all right, but before he could say anything, she was asleep.

Brendan never needed any stimulant; life intoxicated him. He drank deep of it and had a gusto for it all—the simple things of life and the beauty of women and the gallantry of men, the rich splendor of the seasons in New England, the crash and excitement of battle, and the bright face of danger. It followed that he exacted a very high quality of obedience; and men loved him, or hated him, or envied him, and no doubt some feared him: but they were never indifferent.

* * *

1120
Third day

"Better, ma'am?" The corpsman pushed back the curtain of her hair to peer at her face. "You look like you have seen a ghost. Here have a little bit of water."

She shook her head at the proffered canteen full of water and sat up, wiping the damp rag he had brought across her face.

"Are you okay?"

"Yes I'm okay but who are you and where did you come from?"

"We are United States Marines ma'am; and we are suppose to be in Columbia; but we doubt that after today. What is your name?"

"Moira" replied the young woman softly. "You wear strange clothes and carry around funny looking sticks that spit fire."

"I could say the same about you but these are battle fatigues and we are from the year 2005."

"You must be mistaken, this is the year 837 and this is Ireland."

"Yes we know that now but believe me we do not understand why we are where we are."

"What is your name?"

"Jesse Fontenot ma'am" he realized that if he gave his rank and told her he was a Navy corpsman assigned to the Marines she wouldn't have a clue as to what he was talking about so he just dropped that part of the conversation for now.

Their conversation was cut short as the tall rangy captain came back to check on her.

"I have to leave and attend to more serious cases now; but I will come back and check on you again." The corpsman got up and excused himself to the captain.

"Her name is Moira skipper;" as he left.

"Well Moira I see that you are feeling a little better."

Her face was very fair, and her long hair was like a river of gold. Slender and tall she was in tattered gray clothes; but strong she seemed and stern as steel. Thus Brendan for the first time in the full light of day beheld Moira, and thought her fair, fair and cold, like a morning spring that has not yet come to womanhood. And she was suddenly aware of him.

As the initial shock wore off small talk mellowed into the glow of companionship. They continued to talk about the country-side through which the Marines were passing, at first. Then, cautiously, about Brendan, and where he had come from; she was fascinated by Brendan's descriptions of modern life, though he could tell that most of his stories seemed like fairy tales to her. She loved especially the descriptions of automobiles, tanks and airplanes, and made him describe them over and over, as minutely as he could. She believed he came from the land of the fairies.

* * *

When she was well enough to walk, Brendan escorted Moira to Iarnkne's party. When Muirgel first saw them together, she reacted strangely; almost like a jilted lover. Later, when Muirgel realized that whatever the initial bond between Moira and Brendan might be, it was not the sort that made them potential lovers. Brendan treated Moira with great respect. The girl was obviously more than a woman than Brendan was willing to see.

* * *

Road to Meath

At what was latter dubbed the 'battle of the Borne valley', Murphy's Marines had received a shocking introduction to a warrior with strange garb. He was a tough and fanatical foe who often displayed a total disregard for his safety in battle. When defeat seemed certain and escape impossible, he invariably fought to the end, preferring death to surrender.

Joseph Murphy

* * *

1545
Third day

The Marines rested, some settling on logs while others sat on the ground, and they read and reread old letters from home, then committed them to memory for they had begun to fall apart. They thought of writing letters themselves, but the paper was sodden, their pencils had swelled and burst, the ball point pens had become clogged and their points had separated. They pried apart their pocketknife blades which had rusted together and scrapped the mole off their clothing and off their rifles and slung their rifles upside down under their ponchos, while debating whether or not to keep a ruined wristwatch or heave it into the marsh. They removed their precious cigarettes from beneath their helmets and lit them with matches kept dry inside a contraceptive and smoked them with cupped hands. They badgered their NCOs for dry socks or a cartridge belt to replace those now decomposing. They ate hot chow of which the rain made a cold wet slop and they were very grateful for the coffee kept hot in covered GI cans; sometimes so hot that it heated the lips of the drinkers. They went through the motions of pretending this was a bad dream; because if they didn't they would lose their minds.

"You gonna eat your bread?"

Golightly looked up at O'Hare's inquiring face. "Man, I'm sure glad I ain't your mama and gotta feed your big ass. Here." He tossed the slice of bread at the grinning face across from him.

"Thanks, Golightly, but you gotta watch your language. It's getting real bad."

Golightly rolled his eyes back. "Sure, Corporal, I'll work on it for you."

The squad broke up in laughter.

Some birds were active in the bush behind them, a siskin, they supposed or a thrush. They listened to their dilatory rustlings, watched the small fluffy clouds float by, and pondered the etiquette of the situation. They came into a country entirely different and strange to them, where the damp heat of the lowlands sapped their vitality, and the narrow roads, deep with sand-like dirt, muddy along the streams, and winding between forest walls that cut off light and air, were heavy under their feet. They were in a time warp. That said, the next morning they cleaned their rifles, made certain that grenade pins were not rusted tight, checked for extra ammo, and then they got ready to do what they have done so well for so long—FIGHT.

* * *

Anxious to reach Castle Meath before being intercepted by Tuirgeis and his men, Iarnkne, accompanied by several of his new found friends called *Marines*, kept to a fast pace and a grueling schedule. Allowing the main body of Marines on foot to lag behind they made much better time, despite bad roads. Iarnkne along with Brendan pushed them, though, stopping only for the briefest period of rest. In Brendan's eyes, Muirgel needed to get to a place of rest, where the Marine medics could further work on her.

* * *

1840
Third day

Within a few hours the lights of Castle Meath shone through the darkness to welcome them. Muirgel had never thought she would consider the bleak edifice an outpost of advanced civilization, but just now the lights seemed to be those of a beacon of enlightenment.

PART II

War

The second seal is opened and a Red horse appears, its rider holds a sword which signifies bloody War, and the sword held by the rider symbolizes war and violence.

Chapter Eight

Kingdom of Meath

Long, long ago beyond the misty space
Of twice a thousand years,
In Erin old there dwelt a mighty race,
Taller than Roman spears;
Like oaks and towers they had a giant trace,
Were fleet as deers
With winds and waves they made their 'biding place,
These western shepherd seers.
—The Celts

Brendan had a number of vivid memories of his Father describing Ireland in the Roman times "They, the Romans, didn't do much more than skirt the edges of Ireland. The island was wild at the time, and the people were fierce, and they lived in tribes. They were good-looking, of course, even back then but they believed very much in magic, and in the wind and the sky and the power of the earth. They were fine seamen, too." He had listened intently. Good memories flooded back; memories of long summer days spent playing baseball and getting ready for fall football, memories of days when there were no urgencies, no responsibilities, no terrors, just memories of boyhood. In those days he had been eager to hear about battles and knights and sword play never dreaming that he would be taking part in a similar battle. However, he never discussed Genti or Viking times; when you thought about it in one way, a couple of hundred years seemed like an awfully long time. But when you thought about it in another way, it wasn't long at all.

* * *

2010
Third day

Iarnkne sent his gelding into his fastest canter. As he rode, he remembered his vow to himself that if he and Muirgel both survived to reach Meath, he would forgive her for questioning his honor and his word. Then, he'd marry her. The thought teased a laughing breath from him. Alfrey was right; marriage to Muirgel would be like riding an unbroken horse, but sometimes the colts hardest to break tamed in the finest horses.

Foam began to fleck the gelding's mouth. His breath huffed from him in rhythmic snorts. With the landscape now so flat, Iarnkne could watch those behind him and Muirgel try to keep up with them. The Marines being on foot kept moving at their forced march pace.

The dark gates were swung open as they entered the castle. As Iarnkne and his party, including Muirgel and her personal guard, approached an equerry bearing the King's standard rode out to greet them. The travelers then entered, walking in file behind their guide. They found a broad path, paved with hewn stones, now winding upward, now climbing in short flights of well-laid steps. Many house built of wood and dark doors, they passed. Beside the way in stone channel a stream of clear water flowed, sparkling and chattering. At length they came to the center of the castle.

An excited hostler, ran up to Muirgel's horse, and grabbed the halter. "What happened to the princess?"

"We were attacked by Tuirgeis' men" responded Iarnkne as he swung down from the saddle leaving the reins to another youth who had come out to assist.

The rest of Iarnkne's command dismounted and stood streaming in the wet courtyard for another ten minutes before being dismissed.

* * *

Iarnkne made sure Muirgel was attended to first before he left. The still clean scent of his soap filled her nose; she shivered. She was still in pain as he kissed her again; this time very tenderly. A wave of pleasure crashed over Muirgel. With it came the image of bare skin and joy. Despite the pain she leaned into his body. He kissed her and as his lips brushed hers, she gasped quietly then her eyes closed.

The Marine contingent entered the castle awhile later.

* * *

"The lass needs hot tea, not whiskey; hot strong tea with plenty of sugar on it. She looks bloody awful."

"Perhaps a tot of whiskey as well," said Alfrey, neatly removing the cork of the flask as the tea passed and added a generous dollop from it. Accepting the streaming cup gratefully, Muirgel raised it in mute tribute to Alfrey and the rest of her personal guard before cautiously bringing the hot liquid to her mouth. Her hand shook badly, and her handmaiden wrapped her own around her fingers to guide the cup.

More servants were bringing in a portable camp bed, a mattress, more blankets, more bandages and hot water, and a large wooden chest containing the castle's medical supplies.

"I thought we had best work here before we take her to her room and before a fire." The handmaiden explained in her charming bird-like voice. "There is more light, and it's far to the warmest place in the house."

At her direction, two of the larger menservants each seized an end of the blanket under Muirgel and transferred it smoothly, contents and all, to the camp bed, now set up before the fire, where another servant was industriously poking the night banked coals and feeding the growing blaze. The maid who had brought in the tea was efficiently lighting the wax trappers in the branched candelabra; the hand maiden plainly had the soul of a master-sergeant thought Brendan; who had finally arrived with his Marines.

"Shall we help her," asked gunny Smith.

"No gunny let them do their thing, but I am satisfied that with the antibiotics we gave her over the last several hours and the cleansing of the wound our medics did that she should be all right. Let's not be pushing ourselves on them."

"Aye aye sir."

The handmaiden then proceeded to put a leather strap in Muirgel's mouth as she further cleansed the wound; she at one time slowly and deliberately crossed her eyes. This made her look so like an eccentric that everyone broke into half-hysterical laughter. Iarnkne now realized why physicians seldom treat members of their own family. Some jobs in medicine require a certain ruthlessness to complete successfully; detachment is necessary to inflict pain in the process of effecting healing.

It was a long, horrible, nerve wracking job, though not without its fascination. Some parts, such as the probing within the wound to make sure any and all foreign objects were out; and that the wound was thoroughly cleansed.

Muirgel's face was turned away from Iarnkne and Brendan, but they could see the jaw muscles bunch as she clenched her teeth harder on the leather strap. The handmaiden working on her clenched her own teeth and went on to complete the task at hand.

Once finished the handmaidens were guiding Iarnkne and Brendan to chairs next to Muirgel and pressing cups of tea, laced with whiskey, into their shaking hands. Muirgel although exhausted from the ordeal looked over to Iarnkne and said "Are you all right ?"

"Am I all right? My God, Muirgel!" Tears stung his eyelids and he blinked hard, sniffing. She raised her right hand slowly, as though it was weighted with chains and stroked his hair. She drew him close toward her, but Iarnkne pulled away conscious of her near exhaustion and let her fall back to the bed. His hand groped for hers and found it.

Her head lay heavy and her breathing eased at last in drowsy exhalations as she fell off to sleep.

* * *

Once inside the castle, after she was treated, Muirgel's Father, the King of Meath, was introduced to Brendan; he was small and much older then he had pictured. His face was almost lost in white locks and braids, bushy beard and eyebrows. However, out of this mass shone two blue eyes. He looked regal. Beneath a scarlet mantle, he wore one of his finest tunics, a garment made of blue and red velvet with the insignia of the family crest embroidered with precious threads onto its breast. His belt was studded with pearls, the golden chain draped across his chest set with rubies. Resting upon his brow was his crown, the flickering light teasing colored fire from the massive jewels that decorated it.

The King was renowned throughout the land for his kindness and readiness to give refuge to all whose own lands had been torn by strife. Wherever their place of birth, all those who had been persecuted and uprooted dreamed of one day finding succor in his fabled kingdom, and many had their dreams fulfilled.

It was no secret that all who reached the castle brought their customs and habits, and they were encouraged by the King to keep those ways. So the fabled kingdom became a wondrous mix of differences. Bog people mingled with the plainsmen there; seafarers with farmers; mountaineers with forest dwellers. Children growing up in the kingdom at the time were surrounded by a swirling blend of costumes, an array of exotic foods and spices; skills acquired in faraway trades and arts, and travelers' tales of fabulous domains. The Kingdom strength grew from that rich diversity. However that was then and this was now; they now knew they were in a battle for survival and they needed every warrior and weapon they could lay their hands on.

Brendan remembered something about bowing before a king because proper etiquette demanded it. This Brendan did reminding himself as he bent that he really didn't have to do anything.

"My daughter is resting comfortably now but I do want to thank you for saving her life." With that comment the King signaled for wine to be brought to them.

"It was my pleasure" said the still bewildered Marine commander.

Maelsechlainn raised the bell-shaped decanter, with an inquiring cock of one dark brow. As he poured to the proffered glasses, he said "To your health!"

"Now my guest, come!" said Maelsechlainn. "Come and take such refreshments before you retire; for you had terrible ordeal."

Iarnkne heard the heralds crying and the war-horns blowing. The King was assembling men for war.

The King looked at Brendan again and said "I owe you Brendan Murphy captain of Marines. I would give you a gift at your choosing. You have only to name it that is mine, except of course my sword."

"That is very kind of his Highness. As for your gift, Lord, I will like to think about that and choose at a later time, if that be not offensive to you." Brendan didn't care about a gift but did not want to offend the King and his customs.

"Of course captain, you may choose whenever you want."

* * *

"And to you my other guests I will offer such things as may be found in my armory. Swords you may not need, but there are helms and coats of mail of cunning work. Choose from these and may they serve you well."

Alfrey strode across the drawbridge of the moat around the central keep and into the armory on the ground floor. All the arsenal of Meath lay ready. Covered in a heavy layer of dust and cobwebs, the weapons rested since the day they were last put there; longbows and crossbows, spears, pikes and halberds, bolts and arrows of all description. Scores of hauberks and suits of armor also waited for someone to put them on.

The Mystery of the Angels

* * *

0430
Morning
Fourth day

Next morning, roused at daylight by the twittering of birds outside and people inside, Brendan dressed and found his way through the drafty corridors to the hall. Restored to its normal identity as a refectory, enormous cauldrons of porridge were being dispensed, together with bannocks baked on the hearth and spread with molasses. The smell of steaming food was almost strong enough to lean against. Brendan felt still off-balance and confused, but a hot breakfast heartened him enough to explore a bit.

The castle was full, as were the lofts and cubbyholes, the kitchens and the closets.

* * *

Celebration

Brendan concluded that this was an occasion of some importance, and grew more convinced by the extent of the preparations for it. A constant stream of foodstuffs poured into the great kitchens, and more than twenty skinned carcasses hung in the slaughter shed, behind a screen of fragrant smoke that kept the flies away. Hogsheads of ale were delivered by wagon and carted down to the castle cellars, bags of fine flour were brought up from the village mill for baking, and baskets of cherries and apricots were fetched from the orchards outside the castle wall.

Visitors were already beginning to arrive at the castle, though Gunny Smith had heard that the official parts of the celebration would not take place for several days. The more illustrious of Maelsechlainn's tenants were housed in the castle proper, while the poorer men-at-arms and cottars set up camp on a fallow field below the stream that fed the castle's loch.

Joseph Murphy

1500
Fourth day

The banquet was beginning and the King took his place of honor at the head of the table. Brendan glanced down the diner table and across the room. He reflected on the events of the past few days and wondered what Colonel Hull must be doing and thinking at this precise moment. Thinking about Colonel Hull was rather like touching a sore tooth; his initial inclination was to shy away. But the time was coming when he could delay no longer, and he forced his mind back, carefully recalling how excitable he was about the care and welfare of his men. God here was a whole company of Marines missing in a time warp. He must be going bat-shit right now.

Iarnkne arrived with Alfrey and their appearance befitted the knights they were. Iarnkne wore his gray satin tunic trimmed in silver. The garment wasn't as fine as he could afford, however it was suitable to his rank. At his waist was a supple leather belt, its tip encased in silver filigree. His only weapon was a small dagger in silver scabbard. Alfrey, on the other hand, wore all black with the crest of a silver eagle over his left breast.

Dinner was held in a long, narrow room outfitted with tables down the length of each wall, supplied by a constant stream of servants issuing from archways at either end of the room, laden with trays, trenchers, and jugs. The rays of the early autumn's late sunlight came through the high, narrow windows, sconces along the walls below held torches to be lighted as the daylight failed.

Amused at the idea, and to keep his sanity, Brendan looked over the other diners with an eye to spotting ethnic types. As he played the tables, he looked in the opposite direction, toward the next table where Gunny Smith sat, next to Alfrey; a bloody Viking, that one. With his impressive height and those broad, flat cheekbones, he could easily imagine him in command of a dragon ship, deep slunk eyes gleaming with avarice and lust as he peered through the fog at some rocky coastal village. The conversation was general but Brendan could see small groups of visitors talking and looking at the strange creatures among them; the Marines.

The Mystery of the Angels

Banners hung on the walls between the windows, plaids and heraldry of all descriptions splotching the stones with color. By contrast, most of the people gathered below for dinner were dressed in serviceable shades of gray and brown, or in the soft brown and green plaid of hunting clothes, muted tones suited for hiding in the woods; not too dissimilar from the Marines in cammies.

Both Iarnkne and Muirgel, who was rapidly recovering and heavily bandaged, were sitting at the supper table in their respective places in the Great Hall, accepting the toast and good wishes being offered in their honor.

The Marines felt curious glances boring into their backs as young people passed by them, but most of the diners kept their eyes politely upon their plates. There seemed little ceremony here; people ate as they pleased, helping themselves from the serving platters, or taking their wooden plates to the far end of the room, where two young boys turned a sheep's carcass on a spit in the enormous fireplace. There were some several hundred people to eat, and perhaps dozens more to serve. The air was loud with conversation, most of it in Gaelic.

O'Hare rather hesitantly picked up the large horn spoon offered him. He had not been sure what sort of food was likely to be offered, and was somewhat relieved to find that his platter held a row of homely and completely familiar smoked herrings.

Conversation at the tables was limited to occasional request for further food, as everyone settled down to serious eating. Golightly found his appetite rather lacking, partly owing to the shock of the circumstances, and partly to the fact that he really didn't care for herring, when all was said and done. The mutton was quite good, though, and the bread was delicious, fresh and crusty, with large dollops of fresh unsalted butter.

Moira, sitting across and down from him, watched Brendan closely in conversation and touched her hand to her ear, tracing the spot Brendan had touched with his mouth.

"That's a beautiful fire they have tonight, isn't it?"

Startled by the comment from an old woman sitting next to her, Moira tore her gaze from Brendan to look at the dowager, her eyes raised in question. It was Lady Nolan, a plump woman, dressed in heavy gowns of golden threads, no doubt spun by her. Her veil was as thin as Moira's, the silk tissue clinging to her round cheeks. Her bulging eyes were a bright blue. The old lady's lips took a sly twist.

"But I think there couldn't be anything more beautiful than yon man." Mrs. Nolan added at a whisper with a jerk of her head in Brendan's direction.

Moira's heart dropped. There could be no worse calamity than for this old woman, Mrs. Nolan, to discover Moira's true interest in this strange garbed person. The woman would only cry to everyone else that she was pursuing the stranger. This would not bode well for her since she gleaned their might even be an interest in him on the part of Muirgel even though the latter was betrothed to Iarnkne.

"I suppose I'd be less than honest to say he's anything but handsome," Moira said, bringing a cup of wine to her lips for a sip, only to discover it was dry. This meant that Moira had had drained the cup. Setting the vessel back in place, Moira leaned back on the bench she was seating on, and smiled at the old lady.

"If I had a choice between him and the fire I would choose the fire."

Mrs. Nolan continued to push and her dry laugh sounded like a hen's cackle. "A wise choice, I can't speak for you, my lady, but in my life I've learned that a man might burn hot enough to warm me, but his sort of warmth only lasts a little. As for the fire, I can feed the flames until heat penetrates the very stones of my home, keeping me warm throughout the night. That is something no man has ever done for me, at least not without great effort on my part."

What was it she felt for him? She wondered. She liked him, but why; physical attraction? He was good-looking, even if he came from another time-zone. He made her feel good when she looked at him. Her desires suddenly embarrassed her and she quickly looked away.

She had been more than conscious of his attraction. It had happened before, as it doubtless happens to almost everyone. A sudden sensitivity to the presence, the appearance, of a particular man or woman, she supposed. The urge to follow him with her eyes, to arrange for small "inadvertent" meetings, to watch him unawares as he went about his work, an exquisite sensitivity to the small details of his body; the shoulder-blades beneath the cloth of his shirt, the lumpy bones of his wrists, the soft place underneath his jaw, where the first prickles of his beard begin to show.

Infatuation; it was common among people who are thrown together for periods of time into one another's company.

When dinner was finished, the tables cleared, and the room emptied of most of its inhabitants, Brendan stood and paced before the fireplace in the King's castle. Gunny Smith took his leave and saw to it that his men were bedded for the night. Brendan's body filled with tension and energy of barely controlled passion; the fires in him enough to destroy anyone who got too close. The lines in his face betraying his real thoughts. His body was coiled for battle, his face a cold white, eyes angry slits. Autumn's frustrated breath, sucked into the hall by the greedy fire at the room's center, exploded around the wooden panel, holding in its depths the smell of rain and wood smoke from the town outside the castle's walls.

One of the servants seeing Smith groping his way along the corridor, kindly lighted him to his chamber. She touched her candle to the one on the table, and a mellow light flickered over the massive stones of the wall, giving him a moment's feeling of entombment. Once she left, though, he pulled the embroidered hanging away from the window, and the feeling blew away with the onrush of cool air. He tried to think about everything that happened, but his mind refused to consider anything but sleep. He slid under the quilts, blew out the candle, and fell asleep watching the slow rise of the moon.

* * *

0445
Mediation
Fifth day

The chapel was dark except for the burning of the red sanctuary lamp and a few of the clear white votive candles, flames rising straight in still air before the shadowed shrines of saints.

Brendan followed Iarnkne down the center aisle, genuflecting in his wake. Gunny Smith knelt toward the front, head bowed.

The sacrament itself was almost obscured by the magnificence of its container. The huge monstrance, a sunburst of gold more than a foot across, sat serenely on the altar, guarding the humble bit of bread at its center.

Feeling somewhat awkward, Brendan took the seat Iarnkne indicated, near the front of the chapel. The seats ornately carved with angels, flowers, and demons, folded up against the wooden panels of the backing to allow easy passage in and out. He looked up at the crucifix with Jesus hanging from the cross and asked in a low voice "What shall I do? Am I dead?" He sat, listening to his own breathing and the tiny sounds of a silent place; the inaudible things normally hidden in other sounds; the settling of stone, the creak of wood, the hissing of the tiny, unquenchable flames. A faint skitter of some small creature, wandered from its place into the home of majesty. His Mother once described death as "saying goodbye to people on a sailboat. We can only go to the edge and wave to them." The soul was described to him as being like a glove that comes off your hand at death and joins you again in heaven.

It was a peaceful place. In spite of his own fatigue and worry over how he ever got here. He gradually felt himself relaxing, the tightness of his mind gently unwinding, like the relaxation of a clock spring. Strangely he didn't feel at all sleepy, despite the earliness of the hour and the strains of the last few days.

After all, he thought, what were days and weeks in the presence of eternity? And that's what this was, to Iarnkne, Brendan and gunny Smith.

It was in a way a comforting idea; if there was all the time in the world, than the happenings of a given moment became less important. He could see how one could draw back a little; seek some respite in the contemplation of an endless Being, whatever one conceived its nature to be.

And if there was eternity, or even the idea of it, then perhaps all that he was taught was right; all things were possible, including love. But what if it transcended two different time frames?

The Mystery of the Angels

* * *

Upon leaving the chapel, Brendan walked in silence with Iarnkne for some distance before he spoke.

"Let me ask you a question," he said, choosing his words carefully. "If I knew that some harm was going to occur to a group of people, should I feel obligated to try and avert it?"

Iarnkne rubbed his nose reflectively on his sleeve; the allergies were upon him.

"In principle, yes," he agreed. "But it would depend also upon a number of other things; such as what is then risk to yourself, and what are your other obligations? Also what is the chance of your success?"

"I haven't the faintest idea; of any of those things, except obligation of course."

They passed through the kitchen where Iarnkne broke off a piece of pastry and passed it to Brendan, steaming.

"I intervened, as you know on Muirgel's and Moira's behalf. We killed people who might have had children, if we hadn't killed them. I may have affected the future . . . . No I have affected the future; and I don't know how, and that's what puzzles me so much."

"Um," Iarnkne grunted thoughtfully, and motioned to a passing handmaiden, who hastened over with a fresh pastry and some ale. Iarnkne filled two cups before speaking.

"If you have taken life, you have also preserved it; for that I am eternally grateful and am in your debt. How many of the sick you have treated would have died without your intervention? They also affect the future. What if a person you have saved should commit an act of great evil? Is that your faith? Should you on that account have let that person die? Of course not" he rapped his pewter mug on a table for emphasis.

"You say you are afraid to take any actions here for fear of affecting the future. This is illogical, my great warrior friend. Everyone's actions affect the future. Had you remained in your own time frame, your actions would still have affected what was to happen, no less than they will now. You have the same responsibilities that you would have had then-that any man has at any time. The only difference is that you may be in a position to see more exactly what effects your actions have-and then again, you may not." He shook his head, looking steadily across the table they were now seated at.

"You are a Catholic and I am a convert to Catholicism. The ways of the Lord are hidden to us, and no doubt for good reason. You are right that the laws of the Church were not formulated with situations such as yours in mind, and therefore you have little guidance other than your own conscience and the hand of God. I cannot tell you what you should do, or not do."

"You have free choice; so have all the others in this world; and history, I believe, is the culmination of all those actions. Some individuals are chosen by God to affect the destinies of many. Perhaps you are one of those; perhaps not. I do not know why you are here. You do not know. It is likely that neither of us will ever know; but again I am glad you are here." He rolled his eyes, comically. "Sometimes I don't even know why I am here!" Brendan laughed and Iarnkne smiled in return. Iarnkne leaned, toward Brendan, across the table intense.

"Your knowledge of the future is a tool, given to you as a shipwrecked castaway might find himself in possession of a knife or a fishing line. It is not immoral to use it, so long as you do so in accordance with the dictates of God's law, to the best of your ability. And that my friend is all I can tell you; no more."

He shoved the remaining pastry towards Brendan.

"That said whatever you do, you will need strength for it. So take one last piece of advice: when in doubt, eat." Both men laughed.

"I can't tell you what a relief it is to talk to someone about this," Brendan replied picking up the pastry. "And I still can't get over the fact that you really do believe me."

*   *   *

The festivities, despite the threat of Tuirgeis, continued for several days in that kingdom. For there was much to celebrate; the joyous reunion of Muirgel and her Father, the continuance of the reign of Maelsechlainn and the recovery of Muirgel from her wounds. And during that time, Moira had done all she could to put herself in

Brendan's pathway. Although they'd passed each other in the yard and hall time and again, the Marine company commander hadn't responded to a single of her inviting smiles, only eyed her in silence.

Moira was excited. Tonight was the night. Mrs. Nolan, the old woman, who made the comment, told her that all the fighting men would be in the hall tonight, to make their oaths of allegiance to Maelsechlainn. With a ceremony of this importance going on nobody would be watching the Marines; except her and one in particular.

Life seemed to be assuming some shape, if not yet a formal routine. If Castle Meath was a peaceful place, it was also a busy one. Everyone in it seemed to stir into immediate life at cockcrow, and the castle then spun and whirred like a complicated bit of clockwork until after sunset, when one by one the cogs and wheels that made it run began to fall away, rolling off into the dark to seek supper and bed, only to reappear like magic in their proper places in the morning.

At dinner preparations that night, Moira found Brendan slowing working his way toward a door, sidling through folk lifting tabletops and shifting benches. He was leaving she thought to herself. Who knew when her next opportunity to meet with him alone might arise? It was only at public events like feasts and fairs that men and women could interact without winning criticism for their behavior. Damn her arrogance! Brendan wasn't a fool. He wasn't going to let her repay him for what he'd done. She couldn't stand idly by. She had to act and fast. She moved towards a spot that she carefully chose to intercept him.

Brendan froze in admiration. He spotted Moira to his front. By God she was a beautiful woman. What little firelight pierced the dimness gilded her skin and found golden lights in her blonde hair. Her expression was soft, her eyes luminous. There was nothing of passion in her face save the natural sullen curve of her lips. He was about to say something to her as he approached her, but was intercepted by Muirgel who said her Father wanted to talk to him.

Moira was terribly disappointed; but controlled her disappointment as he turned and left with Muirgel. She stared at the oaken floor with a very unpleasant sensation in the pit of her stomach. She was remembering the look of gay anticipation on Muirgel's face as she met up with Brendan. However, for the rest of the night she would be the only thing in his thoughts. And that was really what Moira wanted without knowing it. She wanted him to think of her each and every night until she was the only thing on his mind.

Commoner or gentleman, a man was still a man. Priests taught that females lacked the ability to control themselves and their baser natures, something Moira felt they had backwards until she met Brendan. However, having heard such things all her life and despite what he said to her, deep in her heart did Brendan think her incapable of controlling herself, not just with him but with any man?

Iarnkne was in a side room awaiting Muirgel and Brendan. He somehow looked bigger here. His form filled the doorway, his shoulders nearly brushing the jamb at either side of him. Rather than his gray armor he wore a knee length tunic beneath his dark cloak, this one the red of his family's house, a hue that suited his coloring. His boots reached to his knees, dark garters holding their soft uppers to the line of his calves. His long sword was belted over his tunic, his hat and gloves tucked into the belt.

With no hat to disturb its fall, his dark hair curled lightly against the sharp lift of his cheekbones. Sunlight caught against his clean-shaven cheeks, then gleamed on the narrow of his beard as it followed his jaw. Muirgel smiled. He looked different and it just wasn't his attire.

Muirgel was recovering nicely from her wound and while the married women seemed friendly enough, the younger girls seemed to still resent the fact that she had taken Iarnkne, an eligible young bachelor from circulation. In fact she even noted some cold glances and behind the hand remarks, she wondered just how many of the Castle maidens had found their way into secluded alcoves with Iarnkne. She chuckled to herself and moved among the guests.

* * *

Standing alone

The rider bent low over his mount's neck, lashing the creature hard, as he rounded the bend in the road. He kept looking back as if the winged devils were after him, and he did not notice that there were hundreds of refugees on the road leaving from the village of Rawa. Refugees from that destruction, old men and women with infants, were escaping to safety to the kingdom of Meath. Some were riding in horse drawn vehicles, or farm wagons loaded with household goods, or even carrying babies with the few belongings they could take on this most terrible of voyages. All were visibly downcast, if not in tears. Some pushed the wooden wheelbarrows or rode on horseback, while others were on foot. Shepherds drove their flocks of sheep and goats so as not to leave them for the Vikings. The rider's horse shied in full gallop, lurching sideways so violently that they almost fell. The man cursed and swiped at the peasants with his whip.

"Off the road! Out of the way!"

Horse flesh was expensive. No man drove the wealth of his house across such rough terrain, not when hidden burrows and jutting tree roots might ruin an animal; unless that man was desperate to carry a message and believed he knew the landscape enough to take the risk.

* * *

The man in bearskin cloak stood within the archway, hesitant about entering. He had a silver-gilt brooch as large as the palm of one's hand fastened at the neck. It was made in the shape of two leaping wolves, backs arched and heads meeting to form a circle. His clothes were stained with mud and dust; a traveler or a messenger of some sort. And whatever the message, he had passed it on to Iarnkne, who was even now bending to whisper it in Maelsechlainn's ear.

After gaining his breathe, the messenger said aloud "Some of the barons will not fight with you. They believe Tuirgeis is strong beyond their reckoning. They fear that it is already too late. They believe Tuirgeis will devour everything in his path."

"This is a kingdom of cowards." Maelsechlainn's voice rose as he again indulged himself in another round of outrage over some of his baron's refusals to join in the battle against Tuirgeis. "Maybe they are fearful of Tuirgeis' army but if they ever bare their swords to me, I will squash them like the insects they are."

"Verily," Iarnkne said, now in a loud voice, keen and clear, "to fight is our only hope, and that is also our greatest fear. Doom hangs still on as thread. Yet hope there is still, if we can but stand unconquered for a little while longer."

Slowly Maelsechlainn sat down again, as if weariness still struggled to master him. He turned and looked around at his castle, his daughter and her fiancée. "I will not bend, even in my old age to tyranny. I only regret that these evil days should come to me in my advance age instead of the peace which I have earned."

Iarnkne hearing the news was hot with fury and agitation, and could not keep still, pacing and fuming, looking for something to say. Suddenly he lifted his blade and swung it shimmering and whistling in the air. Then he gave a great cry. His voice rang clear:

"We will follow Maelsechlainn!"

Alfrey and the other knights sprang from their chairs. They looked at their King, and then as one man they drew their swords "We will follow"

Iarnkne stood by his King and turned to his fellow knights "Every man that can ride should prepare to fight. We must destroy Tuirgeis while we have time. If we fail we fall. If we succeed, then we will face the next task."

"This show of support seems good to me," said Maelsechlainn. "Let all my folk get ready! We have faith and hope, but remember Tuirgeis is strong. Other perils draw even nearer. Prepare yourselves swiftly for soon we do battle. I will go to war, to fall in the front of the battle, if it must be. Thus shall I sleep better."

* * *

Decision

Sitting at a long table with Brendan on his right and Iarnkne and Alfrey on his left Maelsechlainn commented to Brendan:

"In the year 795 Vikings raided the island of Lambay off the east coast near Dublin, and from then on there was no respite, it was the start of the present struggle. Sudden and terrifying, the fury of the Northmen struck the monasteries of Ireland at a moment in history when art, literature, and learning had reached their full flower under the patronage of the Church. Soon the country was the victim of pirate attacks on all sides and these first raids were but the preliminary to decades of turbulent years of struggle. The tranquility of Ireland, 'land of saints and scholars', was brutally interrupted by the arrival of the Vikings or Norsemen. They were able to penetrate right into Ireland through their skilful use of rivers and lakes. Enormous treasure, from the palaces and monasteries, was plundered, for the buildings had no defenses; so the monks built round towers in which to store their precious things at the first sign of trouble. Never had the Gaels been threatened like this before."

Brendan although silent nodded in agreement with the King. He remembered from old photographs the construction of those round towers.

Maelsechlainn continued "The Vikings showed more than once that they could defeat the strongest forces that Irish chiefs were able to bring against them and now a messenger brings us news that not all the Irish Kings will join with us in the battle."

Brendan looked up and around the table. He caught Muirgel staring at him. "King Maelsechlainn, please view me as an ally. I pledge my men and arms to support you." There was a low, murmuring from the crowd, but Brendan ignored it and went on "Alpha Company stands beside you in this upcoming battle, which is all you will need." Maelsechlainn, hoping to hear that stood unmoving for a moment, then smiled and held out his hands. After an instant's hesitation, Brendan placed his own hands lightly over Maelsechlainn's palms.

"We are honored by your offer of friendship and goodwill" said Maelsechlainn clearly. "We accept your offer and hold you as a good ally of Meath." The King went on to say "The evening is wearing away. Soon we must go. You have spoken words of hope; but only hope. Hope is not victory. War is upon us and all our friends, a war in which only your mysterious weapons could give us surety of victory for we are hopelessly outnumbered. It fills me with great sorrow and great fear; for much shall be destroyed and all may be lost." He rose and gazed outward, as if he saw things far away that none of them could see. "That said we have no choice but to face down our enemy and see that this deadly peril is removed. Even now, the sands of time are slipping through the hourglass, as it were. We need to make haste in our preparations for battle. Yet if my hope is not cheated, a time will come ere long when I can speak more fully and show you my appreciation."

The honor, the acclaim, the gratitude—these embarrassed Brendan, for he was, after all, a modest and private person; and his Marines had already paid a heavy price.

The King added "Send the heralds forth! Let them summon all who dwell nigh! Every man and strong lad able to bear arms, all who have horses, let them be ready in the saddle at the gate." He then leaned over the table and brought up his cup and drank from it. "Fill up, fill up a toast!"

Moira had maneuvered herself to bring the men in the room refreshments and now stood before Brendan to fill his cup. She paused suddenly and looked upon him, and her eyes were shining. He looked down upon her fair face and smiled; but as he took the cup, his hands met hers, and he knew that she trembled at the touch.

"Hail Brendan, captain of Marines," she said.

"Hail lady Moira!" he answered.

When they had all drunk, the King excused himself to participate in the planning. As he passed Iarnkne he whispered "Who shall I entrust my people with, to rule in my place while I am gone?"

"Your daughter your highness, she is fearless and high-hearted. All love her. Let her be as Lord of the manor in your absence."

"It shall be so," said Maelsechlainn. "Let the heralds announce the folk that the Lady Muirgel will lead them!"

* * *

Brendan had agreed to fight with Muirgel and her Father King Maelsechlainn I, Emperor of Ireland, 'The Great' King of Meath.

"They will attack Dublin."

"Yes, I know and we must be prepared to defend against them. I suggest my men defend the right flank"

"Now is the time to stand and strike the hardest blow yet struck for final victory, home and freedom; the eyes of Ireland are upon you.

May God and the Holy One and Mother Mary go with you and keep you and your men safe." The King intoned solemnly when they were finished.

A battle plan was drawn up whereby Brendan's Marines would defend the right flank, which covered the most exposed avenues of attack against Dublin. As a result, Brendan designed his defenses with that in mind. With barbed wire, axes, shovels, sandbags, and machetes which they had in abundance; his men began building a tight bristling defensive ring. Big trees came crashing down, were chopped into sections and dragged over wide sandbagged holes. More sandbags went atop the logs and over this was planted clumps of grass. In that lush-growing moist atmosphere, the grass quickly took root and the rough-hewn pillboxes took on the appearance of low hummocks. Fields of fire, that is, cleared lanes between the guns and the enemy, were burned out in the grass. Apron after apron of barbed wire was strung until many of the Marine fronts were as wicked laceworks of glittering black wire and tan charred grass.

Tomorrow will be a quagmire, Brendan thought. He tried to sleep, but with the eve-of-battle symptoms familiar to many officers—burning eyes, dry throat and queasy stomach, it was not possible.

*　*　*

Brendan was moving quickly with a handful of his men after having a final conference with the King. Moira was once again there. Brendan told the gunny to take over and to prepare the men to move out.

He turned and faced her. The memory of his lips hovering next to her ear returned. His breath had been fresh, his skin smelled of the day's rain. Sensations again streaked through her out of her control, as they had been at that moment. God help her, but how could that have happened?

"Will you promise me you will take care of yourself?" she asked with tears in her eyes.

"Why?"

To date her only contribution to their relationship had been a smile. Not much to fuel a genuine love affair.

"Because I think I'm fond of you."

"I never liked goodbyes. It's a bad habit, I guess."

Moira stepped closer. "Why does it have to be good-bye? I . . . I would like to." She lowered her head and shifted her feet as if uncomfortable. "Well, I wondered if maybe we could . . . be . . . friends. I would really like to talk to you and . . ." She shook her head. "I'm not doing this too well, am I?" She shifted uncomfortably "Could we see each other again and talk before you have to leave?"

"No. We've got a lot to do before the battle begins. Maybe when we get back, and we will, I'll stop by and see you."

Moira forced a smile, but she knew her questions had been upsetting to him. "Brendan, please come back safe and see me. I would really like that."

Brendan smiled warmly "Sure sweet princess, I will."

Moira laughed at the words "princess" and her eyes filled with tears "Okay"

She watched him turn and disappear, knowing he may never come back and see her again. It didn't matter; she would go and see him. She would find a way.

Moira had watched Brendan disappear. He took with him all the confidence he'd striven to instill in her. For a long moment she stared at the empty roadbed. The wind blasted her, bearing in its depths the low of distant oxen from some nearby farmhouse. On the verge, browned grasses flattened, then rippled back to standing as the gust died. Moira gave a cry and buried her head in her hands. Never in all her life did she want someone to kiss her like she did then. How could this be happening to her and with this strange and peculiar man? Yes, there were other knights at court who piqued her interest, but never one who pierced her barriers and stirred her lusts beyond the control of common senses. She now knew she loved Brendan madly; that was not the problem. She had felt something special the moment he had rescued her; and this spark had almost immediately, almost frighteningly, turned into excitement and desire.

The problem was that they really had no future; and she was fully aware of that. Brendan Murphy was an officer of the United States

Corps of Marines, in the year 2005, about to leave to fight a vicious enemy, almost certain never to return, but even if he did for how long? The mist that brought him here could easily take him back; and she was stuck in the year 837. It was bad enough to see him off to battle wondering if he would live or die but what about the future never knowing? The Viking army was poised to take over Dublin. This might happen in the next few days or in the weeks to come. In any event, it seemed like it would happen, unless a miracle occurred, and when it did she would be at their mercy. So why did she put herself in this utterly hopeless situation?

They had marched out of the gates of Castle Meath, in typical Marine Corps style, just before dawn. In company formation, to the sound of pipes, shouted farewells and the calls of wild geese on the loch, they marched smartly over the stone bridge. They marched in perfect step. Their backs straight, their faces set, the folks gathered, stopped and stood, impressed at the ranks of somber men in camouflage fatigues who wore strange helmets and carried even stranger looking sticks that barked fire. The locals stood a little straighter themselves, with chins held high as the sound of the bagpipes echoed across the burn. They could sense that these strange people from another era were touched by tremendous pride in themselves and in their unit they called the 'Corps'. It showed in their steps, their faces, their unwavering eyes. The marching echelon radiated camaraderie, friendship, confidence. Gunny Smith glanced back from time to time, until the bulk of the castle disappeared at last behind a curtain of shimmering mist. The thought that he probably would never see that grim pile of stone or its inhabitants again gave him an odd feeling.

The sound of the cadence of boots seemed to muffle in the fog. Voices carried strangely through the damp air, so that calls from one end of the long line were sometimes heard easily at the other, while sounds of nearby conversations were lost in broken murmurs. It was like marching through a vapor peopled by ghosts. Disembodied voices floated in the air, speaking far away, then remarkably near at hand.

As Muirgel turned, she looked out across the castle's yard to see Iarnkne and his contingent of horsed riders. The newborn sun pierced the veil of hazy clouds to cast rosy light upon the yellowish stones of Meath's Castle enclosing walls. Dew glistened on the roof and wall, the moisture darkening the yard's hard packed pathways and clinging to the tufts of yet green grass that filled the spaces between the paths. With the fires in the kitchens banked, none of the usual smoke pall hung over the compound. For the moment the only scent was rain-washed air.

Chapter Nine

Maelsechlainn's Daughter

> "You are blood of my blood, and bone of my bone.
> I give you my body, that we two might be one.
> I give you my spirit, until our *Life* shall be done."
> —Outlander

Preparing for Battle

Muirgel gazed at Iarnkne and Alfrey who were riding their horses into the yard bearing raiment of war from the King's hoard. Both men had shucked their casual attire in favor of military dress. Seated atop his massive warhorse, overlaid with gold and set with gems, green, red and white, Iarnkne's mail gleamed like ebony under a weak autumn sun. His head was bare, his mail coif dangling down his back between his shoulder blades. He'd shucked the leather under-cap he wore beneath his mail hood. The day's breeze made free with his hair, lifting the blonde strands. At the gate they found a great host of men, old and young, all ready in the saddle. More than a thousand were there mustered. Their spears were like a springing wood. Loudly and joyously they shouted as Maelsechlainn came forth. Some held in readiness the King's horse.

Iarnkne dismounted. Now, stripping off his steel-sewn gloves, he tucked them into his belt and turned to face his betrothed. God, but she was beautiful. Still dressed in her simple green garment, her eyes flashed gorgeous red fire.

Without realizing it she reached up and touched his chin where he had been slightly injured in the Guada battle and caressed the slight red abrasion mark. Touching him triggered a strange sensation in her that embarrassed her. She quickly withdrew her hand but not before his eyes suddenly looked at her in a way that made her stomach flutter. Iarnkne stood staring at her for several seconds then shook his head, turned around, and began walking back to his horse. In a moment he would be gone to fight.

Iarnkne, please . . . . please don't, her thoughts screamed. Her body seemed to shrivel as her stomach knotted with emptiness and pain. She sat down, shut her eyes, and lowered her head.

She had so much wanted to make up for what she said after he rescued her. She had planned for days on what to say knowing these could be the last ones before the coming storm. Before she knew it, he came back and grabbed her and yanked her up into his arms. He was laughing and holding her tightly as she tensed and struggled to free her hands to hit him, but he suddenly became silent and gently lowered her to the ground. He looked into her green eyes.

"I will miss you dearly," he said.

"I will miss you too." She seemed to be lost in his gaze. "Please take care of yourself and come back to me my knight in shining armor." Fantasies about Iarnkne flooded her imagination like a raging river flooding its valleys at springtime. His strong arms holding her so she could not move. She sighed at his touch, then leaned her head into his caress. He ran the ball of his thumb over the fullness of her lower lip. She shivered, only not in cold this time. Desire's heat rose to stain her cheeks. The passion he knew could stir in her darkened her eyes.

Iarnkne withdrew when Alfrey cleared his throat and stated "We are ready to move Sir Knight."

She hesitated, staring into his eyes. In the murky light, they seemed a pure gold. His features were in shadow, which seemed to emphasize the lean planes and rugged angles of his bone structure. She had been frightened and the one who saved her, caressed her, was now leaving her.

"I don't want you to leave right now."

"Why?"

"Because I want to look at you longer," she said. He was beautifully made, with long, graceful bones and flat muscles that flowed smoothly from the curves of chest and shoulder to the slight concavities of belly and thigh. He raised his eyebrows.

"It is as the Lord wishes." She folded her hands and lowered her eyes like a nun at prayer.

Lightning flashed, thunder sounded closer; the storm outside him and inside too, a storm of hunger.

The trumpets sounded. The horses reared and neighed. Spear clashed on shield. Then the King raised his hand, and with a rush like the sudden onset of a great wind the last host rode thundering off.

Far over the plain Muirgel saw the glitter of their spears, as she stood still, alone before the gates of the castle.

* * *

"Check your weapons, check your ammo then recheck again," Gunny Smith kept repeating those words as he moved across his lines.

Pfc Walter Fry unbuckled his web belt. He took his modified M-16 and inserted a full magazine, then took two of the round M-33 grenades from his ammo pouch and put them into his pant pocket.

Golightly glanced down and saw the grenades.

"You like those type of grenades?"

"Yes Lance corporal, I do. I like the ideas that you can throw it like a baseball. It's got a coil spring in it. When she blows, the spring shatters, sending out hundreds of steel fragments. It's got a kill radius of fifty meters!"

"I know all that crap I just wanted to know why you liked them?"

Fry put the fragmentation grenade back into his pocket. "I played short stop for my high school baseball team. I was pretty good and I had a fairly decent arm. These grenades suit my personality." He grinned.

"Gotcha"

Chapter Ten

Battle of the Liffey

> And when he gets to Heaven
> To Saint Peter he will tell:
> Another Marine reporting, sir-
> "I've served my time in Hell."
> —Epitaph, Flanders Field Gaudalcanal

Tuirgeis came to the north with a 'great royal fleet' of 120 ships, which had some ten thousand or twelve thousand hand-picked men, and which he divided into two divisions. His intent was also to assume the sovereignty of all foreigners of Ireland. He had carefully reviewed the plan of attack, with his generals, which called for him to divide his fleet into two squadrons, one of which would enter the Liffey, while Tuirgeis himself would sail up the Boyne with the other. Tuirgeis, previously checked at the mouth of the Erne and the mouth of the Shannon, planned to establish a stronghold by Dublin (Blackpool) at the ford of the Liffey. His combined fleet would sweep the waters clear of Irish shipping and once accomplished he would occupy enclaves along the Irish coast. From these enclaves small bands of invaders would enter the interior of the country, carrying their boats overland with them when necessary, and would strike out and connect them. Once accomplished, other fleets would follow and the Norse would then make a determined effort to found colonies. Two of those enclaves were the villages of Guada and Rawa.

The Viking attacks had been sporadic, until 837, when Tuirgeis came filled with ambition to establish a great pagan empire and to make himself Lord of Ireland, as his countrymen had made themselves masters of England and Normandy. The Vikings had mastered the great waters by constructing ships powered by sail as well as oars, to venture on the deep sea routes to far lands instead of hugging the coasts or steering by sight from island to island. In their long vessels the Viking captains laid their courses by the changing patterns of the stars.

Tuirgeis was a tall and slender leader, with keen, handsome features, red hair, and a short red beard. His green eyes had a genial twinkle in them that turned readily to anger; his temperament went with his hair.

In 837 as planned, sixty Viking ships appeared in the mouth of the river Boyne, and about the same number arrived in the mouth of the Liffey. The areas beside both rivers were ravaged far and wide. Settlement in Ireland was not a major problem in the eighth century. There were considerable areas that were uninhabited. Those coming in peace usually received a welcome from the Irish. The Viking way of life was not very different from that of the Irish, however, there was one key difference; the Irish were Christian while the Vikings still worshipped a pantheon of pagan gods.

* * *

Dawn
Sixth day
Blackpool

The sun was already rising as they rode, and the light of it was in their eyes, turning all the rolling fields to a golden haze. There was a beaten way, southeastward along the foot hills of the outer mountains, and this they followed, up and down in a green country, crossing small swift streams by many fords; far ahead and to the left Dublin loomed; ever darker and taller they grew as the miles went by. As their riding drew on, the heaviness in the air increased. In the afternoon the dark clouds began to overtake them: a somber canopy with great billowing edges flecked with dazzling light.

* * *

With the two villages razed, according to his Plan of Attack, Tuirgeis prepared to conduct his assault against Dublin; waiting for him was Maelsechlainn. Tuirgeis' faith in his military genius had become so swollen by his string of victories that it had crowded out of his mind virtually all the practical considerations. Nevertheless, the force which he had gathered for the ensuing battle was undoubtedly the most formidable yet assembled. Unfortunately, for the Vikings, the same tactics of annihilation, based upon the element of surprise, that had brought success at Guarda and Rawa were not to be at the battle of the Liffey.

Tuirgeis was still supremely confident in the powerful army he had assembled. He rejected all advice to concentrate his forces and strike at one point rather than attack on a wide front. He clung stubbornly to a broad advance, dreaming of a mammoth double envelopment such as had never before been executed. Still intuitive, still believing blindly in his destiny to be a conqueror greater than the world has ever known.

The two armies formed into straggling lines of horsemen and charioteers on either side of the valley northwest of Dublin. The sun played peek-a-boo with the clouds, blood-red in a smoking haze. The spears and swords of Maelsechlainn's men appeared tipped with fire as the shafts of light kindled the steep faces off the mountains. This strip of Ireland was peculiarly adapted to cavalry fighting. It was a country of fine vistas, with bare, rolling hills and little clumps of trees. There were infrequent open fields, and some flowers, and numerous little streams. The battalions were now arranged and drawn up on both sides, in such order and in such manner, that a four-horsed chariot could run from one end of the line to the other, on both sides. Now on the one side of the battle were the bold hard hearted Genti; surly, pagan; without reverence, or honor, for God or for man. They had for the purposes of battle and combat, sharp, poisoned arrows, which had been anointed and browned in the blood of dragons and toads, and water-snakes of hell and of scorpions and otters to be cast and shot at active and warlike valiant chieftains.

On the other side of that battle were the outnumbered soldiers, of Erin and their new allies. They were a nation of horsemen, accustomed to living and caring for themselves in the open. They operated in their own country. They also had, to begin with, better horseflesh. And they had fairly decent leaders, including King Maelsechlainn who now looked out across the vale.

* * *

Prelude

Brendan had been observing Tuirgeis' movements the previous day with the assistance of his micromechanical flying insects known as micro air vehicles. These were tiny, nimble devices developed at Berkeley California in early 2000 which could surreptitiously spy on enemy troop movements without being detected. As a result of their feedback, he moved his company into position to the right of the Irish line flanking the Irish Sea. He had fixed upon a line about a half a mile long, facing west, between Rawa and Dublin. It was on high ground, traced across fields and pastures that were cut up by country lanes and stone walls. On the left were some trees, and a great grazing field, and a knoll that gave good position for flank guards. The other flank rested on a stream of water where a stone bridge of two arches crossed. The right flank was weak because the stream was fordable. The air was cool and wet and delicious to breathe: a slow soaking rain, a farmer's rain. The light came slowly: there were great trees out in the mist. Just then Tuirgeis' men began chanting what one Marine thought was some kind of ritual. The mist was lifting slowly, the rain was slackening. Moments later, the Viking's came at the Marines, three or four abreast, screaming and yelling with spears lowered in a frenzied charge. Tuirgeis' attack, however, was initiated at long range and presented the Marines with a gratuitous opportunity for annihilation by fire. Tuirgeis' charge rose in fury. Section after section, segment after segment, they burst across the valley to dash against the Irish and Marine lines. They broke it. They came in on holes and gun-pits, running low with pikes and spears outthrust for the kill.

There were tall shapes mingling with the short ones, figures that closed, merged, became as one grotesquely whirling hybrid of struggling limbs for now the battle had become that rarity of modern war, the close—in fight of clubbed rifles and thrusting swords, of fists and knees and gouging limbs. Now there were more tall shapes than short ones, for Brendan had thrown in his reserve headquarters platoon, and the guttural cries of the Vikings were growing fainter beneath the wild keening of the battle, the crackling of the rifles, the hammering of the machine guns, the gargling of the automatic weapons and the thumping whump of the mortars.

The Vikings were stumbling now over heaps of slain comrades strewn along the front and the flanks of the defenders. They were slumping into loose ungainly death, for the Marine fire had been multiplied from the right where the mortars had been swung to their right flank on the beach and trained on the beach side. The last of the Genti were trapped. Marine mortars had drawn a curtain of fire behind them. Bullets ahead, shell burst behind, forward or backward was to die.

Some chose a direct frontal assault where Marine bullets still sought and found them. Some chose to run the gauntlet of guns zeroed in on the beach, peeling off to their left at the barbed wire, dashing through the surf only to be dropped where the incoming tide would roll their bodies and cover them with mud. Others chose the sea. They plunged into the water. They tried to swim back to the north, but their bobbing heads were visible targets for the Marine riflemen who had left their fortified positions and themselves flat to fire from the prone position.

"Line 'em up and squeeze 'em off!" roared O'Hare, striding among his men. "Line 'em up and squeeze 'em off!"

Joseph Murphy

* * *

Center of the line

The attack Iarnkne saw forming on the plain in front of him was the desperate ploy of an adversary unfamiliar with the terrain. The first tactical lesson Iarnkne had learned as a squire was that it was far easier to defend the high ground than to force an assault up the slope. Iarnkne straightened his helmet on his head, and then took his oval-shaped shield from its saddle rest. Trained to that sound, the gelding's head lifted in anticipation. He danced against his rider's new tenseness. With his shield on his arm, Iarnkne slid his sword from its sheath, his gloved hand fitting perfectly into its well worn grip.

With a rattle of armor and harness rings, Iarnkne's command leaned forward in their saddles, ready to deliver their first strokes. In his response to the sound, Iarnkne's mind emptied of all thoughts, even that of Muirgel. He lifted his sword, ready to use the skills of his forefathers.

Tuirgeis imagining the war he let loose, believed that he had no time to waste; for he believed that he who struck the first blow, if he stuck it hard enough, may need to strike no more. So the forces that he had long been preparing he now set in motion; sooner than he intended. Now he looked towards Dublin and knew that very soon his strength would fall upon it like a storm.

It was near dawn, and as the sky turned from gray to pink, the sound of distant yelling changed abruptly. There was a thunder of hooves, and several hundred horses came charging in Iarnkne's direction, yelling in the Norse tongue. The sun's limb was lifting, an arc of fire, above the margin of the world. Then with a great cry the heathens charged from the west; the red light gleamed on mail and spear. The Genti yelled and shot all the arrows that remained to them. Iarnkne saw several of his horsemen fall; but their line held. The full fury of Tuirgeis' attack broke upon the Irish defenders in the center of the line. Out stormed the dense Viking lines of battle, short and thick, section upon section with their spears and swords held high in the air and their deep cadenced shouting. A lean darkish line with a glitter of steel along it, and the streaming battle flags above, shaken out in the early light. Those on horse rode through soft green rounded hills, moving toward death as they rode. The onrushing Genti made a furious, smashing onset on the Irish line. They were immediately repulsed but they formed and charged again. One small band held together in a dark wedge, driving forward resolutely in the direction of Iarnkne. Straight up the slope they charged towards him. These were the faces of foes in battle and each of them remembered their ancient animosities towards each other, and each of them attacked the other. And it will be one of the wonders of judgment day to relate the description of this tremendous onset. Then the Vikings, and the champions of Maelsechlainn, met in one place. There was fought between them a furious unmerciful battle. They began to hew, cleave, stab, and to slaughter, to mutilate each other; they maimed, and they cut comely, mailed bodies on both sides there. That was the clashing of two bodies of equal hardness, and of two bodies moving in contrary directions, in one place. It was not easy to imagine what to liken it to, but to nothing small could be likened the firm thunder motion; and the stout, valiant billow-roll of these people on both sides. And there arose a wild, furious, voracious, screaming and fluttering over their heads. And there arose also the satyrs, and the idiots, and the maniacs of the valleys, and the witches, and the goblins, and the ancient birds, and the destroying demons of the air and of the firmament, and the feeble demoniac phantom hosts.They were screaming and comparing the valor and combat of both parties. Iarnkne moved among his men encouraging them and lending his sword whenever the assault was hot. Alfrey went with him. Blasts of fire from Tuirgeis' rocking throwing machines leaped up at them. Again and again the Vikings gained the front slope of the hill, and again the defenders cast them down.

  Close to two hundred Vikings were killed or wounded during the first two hours at the wire, at the expense of three Marines killed and 10 wounded. It had been so one-sided that Brendan refused to believe that it had been a well planned attack with the intention of turning McMillan's seaward flank.

Death of a Knight

Iarnkne's horse fell and he was thrown out of the saddle. He found himself surrounded by plunging hooves and singing arrows. He scampered for safety and in the process slashed at the hamstring of a Genti who had Alfrey cornered. The man dropped to his knees and Alfrey ran him through.

"I owe you a debt of gratitude!" Alfrey shouted.

"Things go hard, my friend," Iarnkne said, wiping the sweat from his brow with his arm.

"Hard enough," said Alfrey, "but not yet hopeless, while I have you with me. Where is the King?"

"I do not know," said Iarnkne. "I last saw him fighting on our right flank."

Roaring like a bull, Iarnkne fought his way out of the mud and dashed headlong into a squad of Genti who had linked their shields together and were now advancing, a formidable human machine, threatening the flank of Muirgel's personal guard. Straining mightily, Iarnkne broke the linked shields and slashed at those behind them. Their awful wail rose above the clamor and drew Tuirgeis' attention from across the field of battle. His gaze locked with Iarnkne's.

Tuirgeis made his way towards Iarnkne and in the process encountered Alfrey who had his hands full with one of his men. Tuirgeis took advantage of Alfrey's blind side to pierce his shield with his sword and cut him on the arm. Alfrey then turned and fought Tuirgeis like a mad-man. Finally it was Alfrey who stumbled and fell. He raised himself to his elbows only to fallback in the mud. For the first time he felt the stabbing pain. The sword had passed through his hip. His right hand, in the mud at his side, lay in a pool of blood. He forced his hand to his hip to feel the entry wound, but instead his fingers touched his scabbard just below the oozing wound. His hand slipped back into the warm crimson pool. His eyelids began heavy. He fought to keep them open, knowing that if he allowed them to close he would never open them again. The pain was now gone. He could feel nothing as he stared at the trees far above him and the endless sky.

Generations, centuries afterward, would record the fight to wild eyed youngsters: how Tuirgeis fought like a demon possessed, raining blows so thick and fast on the Irish that his arms blurred and his axe struck fire off the stones. How Alfrey fought bravely under that savage attack ducking, weaving, striking, until at last Tuirgeis maneuvered him to the top of a slope and forced him down. How Alfrey lost balance and life in that slimy place, hacked by Tuirgeis' ax, and pierced by Tuirgeis' sword. How Tuirgeis kicked him without honor and Iarnkne seeing this last act, hurled his sword spear-like into the antagonist he was facing and ran to his old friend . . . . too late. After that events came so thick and fast that he would never remember them clearly, or remember their proper sequence. For him the battle was a night-terror, a livid and horrible dream. Bolts and arrows sang around him, nipping at his clothes, ricocheting off the stone walls, thumping into the hard wood of the mangoes. He reeled back scrambling for the cover of the battlement that was erected as the Genti attacked. Then he was off, sword flashing, taking steps two at a time, rushing out in front of the Irish lines.

"Back off you focking sod!" He swung his sword like a battle axe missing one Viking. Dauntless he continued on shrieking at the top of his lungs, raw with cold air, howling like a wolf.

The next moment he scored a hit on a Viking who was concentrating on one of Iarnkne's men. The Genti screamed and seemed to convulse. An arrow passed within a foot of him and he caught the tiny blur of its motion before it thudded home into the chest of a Viking about to impale him from his blind side. The heathen died where he stood.

Some could compare the battle to the variegated, boundless, firmament that had cast a heavy sparkling shower of flaming stars over the surface of the earth; or to the startling fire-darting roar of the clouds and the heavenly orbs, confounded and crashed by the winds, in contention against each other; or to the summit of heaven, or to the rapid, awfully great sea, and the fierce, contentious roaring of the four transparent, directly opposing winds, in the act of breaking loose from the order of their respective positions. Or to the stern terrific Judgment-day that had come, to confound, and break down the unity of the four surrounding elements, to crush and finally shiver the compact world, and to take vengeance on it.

Maelsechlainn's catapults cut loose. Several men screamed and crumbled like dolls, but others still came on, driven by Tuirgeis behind them. Many were cast down in ruin, but many more replaced them, and Vikings sprang up like apes in the dark rims of the African continent. Dozens died from booby traps and arrows from crossbows. Still they came; they were upon the Irish lines thrusting and jabbing as in swordplay. Iarnkne lunged back and forth; his armor shone and the plumes on his helmet waved above the Genti troops. His tunic was so dark a gray that it was almost the hue of his armor. Silver embroidery glistened from its neckline and sleeve, the trim modest considering what festooned the garments of his kin-folk. The dead and broken were piled like shingle in a storm; ever higher rose the hideous mounds, and still they came.

The Marines went forward. They sloshed through grass and mud up to their calves and broke into a silent marsh. They slogged on. The Genti sent up reserves to counterattack. The Marines met them in toe-to-toe, tree—for-tree fighting that ended in extermination of the counter-attackers. So it went throughout this bleak, grim day and through the following day, when a fierce charge through a shower of grenades brought death to many of the Vikings.

* * *

Moira packed a supply of bandages on the back of her horse and swung up onto the saddle. She then drove her horse to the place of combat, heedless of the dangers. She just wanted an excuse to be by Brendan's side.

* * *

Brendan had no pity for the Vikings, but he did now. He had pity for the poor wretches caught directly by the blast from the Marine flamethrowers. They changed to white ash, whirled away by the wind. He had pity for those who lived an instant or two, whose skin bubbled and writhed as if there were living creatures under it. Most of all he had pity for those whose clothing was ignited by that fiery jelly, who spent the last moments of their lives shrieking and rolling in the dirt.

"Down! Get down!" he pulled her behind a buttress just as the gout of flames smashed into it, spilling around it, sucking away all oxygen. Both fell gasping to their knees. A strong wind blew the flame of the flamethrower away from the attackers and to the side they were standing. On and on went the blast from the mouths of the flamethrowers, roaring like a hurricane across a mountain tunnel. When it ended, more screams of agony echoed around them as men and horses shriveled to crisp and unrecognizable shapes. For a split second in that chaos, Moira's eyes held Brendan's and her hand touched his arm. She was assisting as a volunteer corpsman for the Marines. Her sole purpose was to be at Brendan's side.

"Don't ever do that again!" He screamed at her.

"But your arm is bleeding," she cried. She delicately tore his fatigue jacket away from the wound. His blood was flowing rapidly, mixing with the mud.

"I have to stop the bleeding." He ignored her plea; kissed her hard on both lips and was on his feet in a flash leading his men. There wasn't an ounce of excess flesh to mark Brendan's powerful frame. His legs were long, his stomach flat. Against the backdrop of the burning fires, she could see his masculine planes. How much she loved him. The thought of him turned her bones to water.

Nothing could compare to the smashing, starry onset of the Irish, under the stout bright axes of the stern murderous, Genti, mutilating, and crushing them. The gleaming, straight swords of Maelsechlainn's men, in powerful clashes against the protective armor of the piratical heathens; smashing the bones of their bodies and their skulls, so that the sound of them, and the uproar of them, and the echo of them were reverberated from the caverns, and from the cliffs, and from the woods in the neighborhood. It became a work of great difficulty to the battalions on both sides to defend their clear sparkling eyes, and their flushed bright cheeks from the heavy showers of fiery sparks.

Joseph Murphy

* * *

Marine Positions
Sixth Day

Gunny Smith whipped out his modified M16 to help cut down the charging Vikings who were only forty yards away. But after three or four rounds, the new M16 jammed like its older models did in Vietnam. Smith quickly dropped to one knee and cleared the weapon and loaded another magazine, it jammed again. Frustrated the old sergeant angrily flung the weapon at the screaming Vikings and unlimbered an old 9mm Browning pistol the P-35, dropping a few Vikings bearing down on him. He would explain later to his Skipper that "Lucky I always carried a personal weapon." The P-35 was special. Its extended, modified barrel also allowed for a small cylindrical silencer to be screwed on in seconds when needed. The holster, he wore, held the silencer in a kid-glove compartment sewed to the outside. Smith pushed the clip release. What was left of the thirteen—round clip fell into his hand. He quickly inspected the green-tipped bullets. They, like the weapon, were special. They were subsonic, loaded to ensure they didn't exceed 1,088 feet per second. Bullets that exceed 1,088 feet break the sound barrier and give the telltale crack. These were quiet although it didn't matter now.

Gunny Smith was unconscious before he had any idea what had happened. One second he had been standing, listening to the yells and the firing, and the next there was nothing at all; no sound, no pain, just blackness. What seemed like eternity but in reality only minutes, Smith shook his head violently to clear it, but the noise went on. He stumbled to his feet and staggered somewhat towards his men. The sounds of battle were still ringing all around him, making his teeth ache and his head spin. His vision began to blur.

The Genti came by the thousands, so many of them rushing and shrieking that the soggy ground shook beneath their feet. They hit the barbed wire even as the Marine guns erupted, and some of them came through it, using the bodies of fallen comrades as ladders over and bridges through the wire.

The barbed wire barrier, erected some thirty yards in front of the Marine line just the day before, however played an important role in stopping and slowing the Viking attack. They came flowing across the open field, sprinting, hurling spears, howling. They came blundering into that strand of barbed wire, and there they milled around in a jabbering frenzy. They hacked wildly at the wire with pikes and swords. Apparently with so many of their comrades falling at or near the wire to the Marine fire, some of Tuirgeis' men cautiously examined the wire believing it was bewitched. Then the Marines opened fire; machine guns chattered and shook. Rifles cracked. Grenades whizzed and boomed. Mortars bayed in the rear distance from the weapons platoon and their whistling shells crashed and flashed among the charging horde and were falling with that dull crunch that tears and kills. But the barrier did not stop all of Tuirgeis' crack warriors. Vaulting or circumventing their way past the obstacle, small groups of Vikings engaged the Marines in hand-to-hand combat. Some Vikings held their razor sharp axes in their hands and used them like baseball bats. Lance Corporal Golightly was in the thick of the fight at the apex of the left flank, firing his modified M-16 until it jammed. Rolling on his back, Golightly was tending to his faulty weapon when a Viking jumped into his foxhole and began stabbing one of his legs with a spear. Astounded, Golightly kicked and jammed the Viking against the wall of his foxhole, freed the jammed bolt, and pumped five quick rounds into the attacker. Private William Tapia picked up his M-60 machine gun to spray a hosing fire. A single Viking hurled a spear that found Tapia's heart. Tapia froze on the trigger. Dead he fired 30 more rounds. Private Ronald Williams picked up the gun, adjusted the belt and resumed fire.

The Viking charge rose in fury. Section after section burst from the covering darkness of the reverse slope to dash across the valley floor and smash into the Marine line. They broke it. They came in on holes and gun-pits, running low with spears outthrust for the kill. At a gap in the leftward wire, several Vikings rushed for Corporal Terry Weddle in his foxhole.

But even as they charged they heard the screaming of shells coming closer, like a wind rushing in from the distance. They wavered and looked overhead, then sudden and terrible the shells began to fall amongst them. All that heard that sound trembled. Many of the heathens cast themselves on their faces and covered their heads with their hands.

Marine mortars began falling among them. Shells flashed along the trails. The Vikings charged and the mortars stayed with them, whittling this heaviest of all charges before it reached the wire. Tuirgeis' men had at last made a direct attack. The Marines pulled pins and threw. They grasped grenades in both hands and tore out the pins with their teeth and arched the lethal bombs toward the onrushing horde

"Fire!" O'Hare bellowed, but he needn't have, nor could he have been heard above that sudden eruption of sound and light. All of his guns were hammering, spitting orange flame. But the enemy was swarming in. It was hand to hand. O'Hare could see Golightly down on one knee, wounded trying to fight off three charging shapes. O'Hare shot two of them with his rifle. The third bayoneted Golightly wounding him and O'Hare killed the third.

The Vikings moved into the gap in the center. O'Hare ran to his right, hunting for men to counterattack the Vikings, for another machine gun to put into the center. He found two machine guns manned by William Lee and Robert Lein.

"Guns up; follow me!" He led them back to drive the enemy out of the center.

Dale Bennett swung his modified M-16 toward them. It jammed. The Vikings rushed onward, screaming. One of them drove downward for the thrust. Bennett seized his open entrenching tool and slashed. The man sank to the ground, his entails slipping through his clutching fingers. The others slowed. Bennett leaped from his hole and attacked, hacking them to death with his thick-bladed tool.

In the din of battle, disorientation was common as both sides grappled in close range combat. Pfc Edward Massey was in the thick of the battle. Having expended all of his ammunition on the enemy at the peak of the battle, Massey helped to evacuate the wounded. While dropping some of the wounded off at an aid station, in the rear, he discovered a small cache of vitally needed ammunition and hauled it back to his old position to rejoin the fight. He fired on Viking targets, once again exhausting his supply of small caliber bullets.

Henniger, kneeling in his muddy gun pit, got on the phone to the Company's mortar section and relayed firing orders.

"Drop it five zero and walk it back and forth (left and right) across the forward slope," he said. With the mortars only a few hundred yards away those fighting on the slope could hear the mortar crew chiefs barking orders "Load, Fire!" A few minutes later Henniger screamed into the phone "Perfect, stay on them. It's knocking the hell out of them!" The cracking of rifles, the hammering of machine guns, the gargling of the automatics, and the jumping wham of the mortars continued all along the line.

During the initial attacks, other groups of Vikings made it across the barbed wire barrier, seizing a few Marine positions in the middle of the line. Exhausted from digging and patrolling during the previous day, some Marines were still dozing in their foxholes when the Viking's attacked. One Marine corporal was stabbed through the face while he slept by a spear-waving Viking. Another Marine in the foxhole, Pfc. William Dalton, woke up in time to grab his weapon but the rifle's safety was on. All that Dalton could do was parry the enemy's blow, in the process of receiving a badly lacerated hand. Mastrion, the platoon leader, a tough man of hard jaw and soft voice, of smiling lips and large cold unsmiling eyes, quickly jumped into the foxhole and plunged his razor-sharp K bar into the enemy's stomach, dropping him to the ground with his bloody entrails squirting out between his fingers. Some of the other Vikings seeing what happened started to back away when a series of shots rang out from another Marine a short distance away, dropping them in their tracks.

O'Hare and Murphy were rallying their men with insults and taunts, trying to drive them forward with those irrational shouts which often halt those rational drifts to the rear.

The tall corporal yelled "Do you want to live forever?" It had been snarled by Dan Daly at Belleau Wood and had been mocked by a generation before it was flung into American teeth again at the battle of Guadalcanal. Now generations later it was being used once more; and it could still sting. Brendan called for more mortars. The shells came whistling in from Roberts platoon. They fell in a curtain of steel not 200 yards in front of them. They shook the Marine defenders, squeezed their breath away, but they made a flashing white slaughter among the Vikings.

When the Viking commanders energized their warriors for attack Brendan marked them and directed redoubled shelling on the enemy breaking for the valley. They were blown apart. The night was hideous with their screams, and those who passed that dreadful line were either cut down by Marine fire or beaten to death by clubbed rifles and bayonets.

* * *

"Attack," cried Maelsechlainn and with a cry and a great noise his horsemen charged. Down from the crest of the slope they came and swept the enemy in front of them through the valley floor. Behind them came Maelsechlainn's foot soldiers with stern cries issuing from them, driving forth the enemy; and ever the sound of blowing horns echoed in the valley.

The Viking hosts roared, swaying this way and that, turning from fear to fear. Again the horns sounded. Down through the breach in the Genti lines charged Iarnkne and his men. The horse riders were upon the enemy and this terror filled the heathens with madness. They fell on their faces before the onslaught; but Maelsechlainn's men showed no mercy.

* * *

Clouds drifting overhead had become suffused with the light of flare and gun-flash. They illuminated the battle as though it were being fought upon a theatrically lighted stage, and all that flashed and glittered and shone to be magnified by the encircling darkness. There was that quality of slow majesty attendant upon night action when two forces move at great speed over great bodies of land mass. Mortar salvos striking the earth threw up great geysers; of earth, they seemed not to leap but to gather themselves upward, to rise in slowpluming fountains, to catch the red light of burning flesh or wood, the red-gold of flame-throwers spewing its liquid death, to make it dazzling with its own phosphorescence and then to burst apart in a million vanishing sparkles.

It would have been an unreal world, a ghostly one, fantastical, but for the pungent smell of smoke, the constant thundering of the mortars and the crashing of grenades and crying of the stricken.

* * *

0800
Counterattack
Morning
Sixth day

Four of Tuirgeis' brigade commanders were killed, numerous section commanders perished and half of his junior officer corps was destroyed; and still the heathens counter-attacked. They came screeching up the hillside full into O'Hare's machine gun sections spitting orange flame a foot beyond their flash suppressors. Short shapes fell, but more came swarming in. It was hand-to-hand. O'Hare saw little Wilkinson down on one knee fighting off three attackers. O'Hare shot two of them. The third killed Wilkinson with a pike, but O'Hare killed the killer. Lance corporal Ranney's gun was knocked out. And sargeant Boyd fought a Viking section leader, parrying sword swings with his rifle, until the rifle was hacked to pieces. Then Boyd kicked at the blade. Unaware that part of his leg was cut away, he kicked high and caught the Viking chief under the chin and broke his neck.

All over the slope the short shapes and the tall shapes flowed, merged, struggled, parted, sank to the ground or rolled down the hill. Everywhere were the Marines voices crying "Kill! Kill!" the gurgling whoops of the Vikings shouting in a foreign tongue screaming.

Then the short shapes flowed back down the slope and O'Hare ran to make sure his M60 gunners had ammo and were ready to resume again. He helped pry open ammo boxes and helped distribute belt links for the guns. They had to be ready for the next charge.

Yelling again, the short shapes came barrel-assing up the forward slopes once more. They could not force the left of the line where Nichol's platoon still held out, though all were wounded to some degree. In Mastrion's center they hit Henniger, O'Hare and Golightly. They moved through the gap, O'Hare dashed to his right to find a gun to stop them he found Mendoza and Mixon beside their gun protected by a fire team of riflemen.

The fight raged on through the wind-whipped darkness, until in the morning, it had come to the end usually foreordained when several hundred lightly armed men charges a force with vastly superior firepower holding a defensive position.

Again the mortars cut off retreat for those infiltrating Vikings, and the Marines went about the work of destroying them. At four o'clock in the morning with the moon in all its glory, some 300 more Vikings launched a counterattack which broke upon their own backs.

They flowed up against the Marine lines yelling and jabbering, and for some time there seemed to be too many of them. Lieutenant McMillan telephoned Captain Murphy and yelled "We're killing them as fast as they come at us, but we can't hold much longer. We need reinforcements!" There wasn't much time for reinforcing them; there was only time for what Murphy was sternly commanding"

"You've got to hold!"

Mortars fell within 75 yards of the front lines, McMillan and his men fought with rifle, bayonet and grenade. By five o'clock the frenzied charge was shattered. There were 200 dead Vikings within the Marine lines. There were more torn and broken corpses out where the mortars had fallen.

"Let's go" cried Brendan, and Alpha Company swept forward with crackling rifles. The attack gathered momentum. It raced forward 150 yards within a matter of minutes. The Vikings resisted with characteristic stubbornness. Nevertheless, they fell steadily backward in the face of a slow, grinding, overwhelming Marine assault supported by flamethrowers and mortars. Finally the Vikings could only turn and run.

On their right, at the southernmost beaches, the Marine assault had split up into squad-to-squad battles. Lieutenant McMillan had led his platoon with the water on his direct right flank. A Genti chieftain rushed him, swinging his sword. McMillan parried with his carbine, jumped back and shot his assailant dead. A Marine fell and McMillan seized the man's M-16. With other Marines he closed on three Genti warriors, his rifle jammed as he drove in slashing with the bayonet. He finished off the enemy.

So the battle raged, moving steadily from the outskirts of an empty village toward the water's edge as the Marines tried to turn the Viking's flank. The Marines and Vikings fought each other among bleating goats, lowing oxen, mooing cows and scampering clucking chickens. Soon the Viking warriors began to fall back behind the razed village and then the Marine Mortar fire increased.

It was like a science fiction movie; full of knights of old, horse drawn vehicles, and great battles. The fight in the end was for victory of right over evil. Brendan thought "good and evil have not changed since yesterday year; nor are they one thing among Vikings and old Irish and another among modern man. They continued in battle array, and fighting from sunrise to evening; the same length of time as that which the tide takes to go, and to flood, and to fill. For it was at full tide the Vikings came out to fight the battle in the morning, and the tide had come out to the same place again at the close of the day, when the Vikings were defeated. The tide had carried away their ships from them, so that they had not at the last any place to fly to, but into the sea; after the mail-coated Vikings had all been killed by Maelsechlainn's force. An awful rout was made of the Vikings, and their Irish allies so they fled simultaneously; and they shouted their cries of mercy, and whoops of rout, and retreat, and running. But they could only fly to the sea, because they had no other place to retreat to, seeing they were cut off between it and the head of Dubhgall's Bridge, and they were cut off between it and the woods on the other side. They retreated therefore to the sea, like a herd of cows in heat, from sun, and from gadflies, and from insects; and they were pursued closely, and rapidly. Marine bullets still sought and found them. Some chose to run the gauntlet of guns now along the shore and those that escaped the bullets were drowned in great numbers in the sea, and they lay in heaps and in hundreds, confounded, after parting with their bodily senses and understandings, under the powerful, tremendous pressure with which the men of Meath, the Marines, and as many as were also there of nobles of Erin, pursued them.

The liquid fire of the flamethrowers began to describe its fiery arc-disappearing as it extended towards the water.

* * *

Many Vikings ran for the sea toward their only avenue of escape, but most were felled by small arms fire before they reached the beach. Their heads which looked like small dark dots to the Marines were difficult targets to hit as they bobbed up and down in the surf, but the Marines relished the targets and picked them off with well aimed rifle fire. A group of 15 Vikings rushed to the water Sergeant Richard Harris began firing at them. He was joined by another Marine. They killed them all and advanced on another group. A terrified Viking burst toward the water and Harris leaped on his shoulders and finished him with a knife thrust. It was that kind of fighting; savage, close, primitive.

* * *

At five o'clock in the evening a dusty, sweating Marine waded into the sea and stopped to bathe his face in the cool water. The Vikings had been beaten back.

* * *

A survey of the battlefield the next day revealed a horrific sight. At the beach edge Brendan witnessed a grisly scene; he saw small and large clusters of Vikings sprawled about in various poses of death. Many of them, partially buried along the water's edge, looked "puffed and glossy, like shiny sausages."

Maelsechlainn and Iarnkne rode the whole of the front line. Light grew brighter about them. Shafts of the sun flared above the crest of the hills, as they gazed down upon the valley floor. The carnage in the valley was even worse.

Hundreds of Vikings lay sprawled about, their bodies horribly mutilated. They were caught in attitudes of flight as though they had been cut down while running for safety. They lay in huge shell holes and in ruined stone houses packed like swarming flies. Some had been caught crawling and clambering, seeking to escape. About them gaunt denuded rocks stuck out of the ground in rows and the buildings they had held were heaped about them in rubble. There was nothing left, only a handful of birds atop a still standing thatched roof.

* * *

The next day Gunny Smith was feeling a lot better and considerably more alert. He thought he had been out for a long time; he showed no symptoms of concussion or other ill effects from the blow; save a sore patch on the base of the skull. He would have gotten up but the medic disapproved of it. The sky was a deep, pure blue, with only a few puffy cumulus clouds floating around in it. Pines lined the road, and Smith relaxed a little.

That afternoon, Maelsechlainn's men prepared to depart. The work of burial was then but beginning; and Iarnkne mourned for the loss of Alfrey; his closest friend and cast the first earth upon his grave. "Great injury has been done to me and this land called Ireland," he said; "and I will remember it until I die."

The King then chose men that were unhurt and had swift horses, and he sent them forth with tidings of victory into every village of the Kingdom of Meath. They bore his summons also, bidding all men, young and old, on the second day to come in haste to the castle of Meath.

"Skipper isn't that a bit premature?" asked Smith.

"Yes, you are right gunny. We have won, but only the first victory in the battle. The outcome of the war has still yet to be determined."

Joseph Murphy

* * *

Maelsechlainn, with Iarnkne beside him, rode up the hill into the walls of Castle Meath. Behind him his horse riders and behind them his foot soldiers and their Irish allies. The Marines pulled up the rear. The people of Meath were cheering. Pipes and drums were blaring a royal welcome, banners on the walls and buildings fluttered in the autumn breeze.

* * *

It was August; days were still long in Ireland. Only a few hours of real night settled on the earth before the gray morning returned. In the valley, the early fall is the loveliest season of the year. The air is like wine, and smells of peat, and in the afternoon the hills lie softly under thin, golden sunlight, their contours molded by the lengthening shadows.

"Chow time," Lance corporal Thomas Puccini whispered. "Where's the chow?"

They had one can of Spam and also a can of peaches "borrowed" from a rear-echelon galley on their march south to the ridge. The man carrying the peaches stumbled and lost the can as it rolled down the ridge into the valley. There were fierce coarse things hissed at him and it was well for the loser of the peaches to veil his face. Puccini opened the can of Spam, tore the soft meat in pieces and pressed them into outstretched hands the men ate.

Others had Lurps, named after Long Range Reconnaissance Patrol. They sat back on their rucks and meticulously arranged them in a neat row. First the foil bag with the freeze—dried food, then a white plastic spoon, two cornflake bars, the toilet paper, matches, coffee, cream, sugar, and Stimulants. They took out their canteens and reached into the right ruck pockets for Tabasco sauce.

This time warp was in many ways still unreal to Brendan; something from a play or a fancy-dress parade. Compared to the sights of high-tech warfare, even modern guerilla warfare he had come from, the massed pitched battles he had seen—men armed with swords, pikes, crossbows and spears seemed picturesque rather then threatening to him.

He was having trouble with the scale of things. A man killed with a cross-bow was just as dead as one killed with a mortar. It was just that the mortars killed impersonally, destroying dozens, even hundreds, of men, while the cross-bow was fired by one man who could see the eyes of the one he killed. That made it murder, it seemed to him, not war. How many men to make a war? On the other hand was it so different from what he and his men did in counter-guerrilla warfare? The Vikings and the early Irish; to Brendan they were no more than names on a chart on the schoolroom wall. What were they, compared with an unthinkable evil like Saddam Hussein or Osama Bin Laden? It made a difference to those who lived under the warlords whether Norseman or Irishman, he supposed, though the differences might seem trivial to him. Still, when had the right to live as one wished ever been considered trivial? Was a struggle to choose one's destiny less worthwhile than the necessity to stop a great evil? He shifted irritably.

They had beaten the Vikings back. The line had held. However, neither side could claim decisive victory, however, for the fog of war which so often obscures which way the tide of battle is flowing had enshrouded the battlefield; but if Maelsechlainn could not be sure that his defense would hold Tuirgeis was beginning to doubt that he could maintain his offensive.

Poker games, in keeping with Marine tradition, started up. O'Hare sat on the ground playing cards, with Henniger, the RTO, several other members of his squad and Golightly.

Henniger threw down two cards. "Gimme four."

"You only put down two," protested Golightly.

"I know, but I Need four to beat your ass." Henniger glanced up and saw Brendan, "Shit, sir, did we disturb you?"

"No not all; I'm just wound up. You should get some sleep though."

"Beg pardon sir but us old salts never sleep; plus I want to beat this gyrene's ass."

Brendan winked at Golightly. "How much does he owe you so far?"

"About twenty bucks, sir."

"You could never play cards, Henniger. You better get some sleep before you go broke."

Everyone broke up laughing as Henniger blushed.

* * *

When Maelsechlainn was asked to describe the battle to his new found friends, those who would not fight with him, he said "I never saw a battle like it, nor have I heard of its equal. And even if an angel of God attempted its description, I doubt if he could give it. But there was one circumstance that attracted my notice there, when the forces first came into contact, each began to pierce the other. There was a field, and a ditch, between us and them, and the sharp wind of autumn coming over them towards us. It was not longer than the time that a cow could be milked, or two cows, that we continued there, when not one person of the two hosts could recognize another, though it might be his son or his brother that was nearest him, unless he should know his voice, and that he preciously knew the spot in which he was; we were so covered, as well our heads as our faces, and our clothes, with the drops of gory blood, carried by the force of the sharp cold wind which passed over them to us.

And even if we attempted to perform any deed of valor we were unable to do it, because our spears over our heads had become clogged and bound with long locks of hair, which the wind forced upon us, when cut away by well-aimed swords, and gleaming axes; so that it was half occupation to us to endeavor to disentangle, and cast them off. And it is one of the problems of Erin, whether the valor of those who sustained that crushing assault was greater than ours who bore the sight of it without running distracted before the winds or fainting."

* * *

Tuirgeis, on the other hand, once wrote "The Irish attach no importance to castles, they make the woods their stronghold and the bogs their trenches." The Vikings experienced what the Germans experienced in World War I and why the Germans nicknamed the Marines "Teufelhunden" or "Devil Dogs."

* * *

Burial with Honors

"They died on a dirt field in an unnamed valley. They will be buried with honors in a place people will ask why. It will be difficult to console those loved ones in their grief with words of *duty, honor country*. Even if we had a folded flag it would be little consolation to a mother or a wife. But you men standing here understand love of country. It is not a love for a land called America. It is the love of men in your Corps who represent her. You know what it is to do your duty—twenty four hours a day for the three hundred and sixty-five days you spend living, laughing, crying, and sharing. They died, Marines, for you and me. They died protecting their friends to their left, to their right or the ones behind them. They did their best so more like them wouldn't fall.

No, Marines don't die for great causes or countries far away. They march forward and give their lives for their friends and fellow Marines, who they know would do the same for them."

Brendan paused as a piper stepped forward and brought his wooden piece to his lips. The shrill refrain echoed through the quiet burn. Its sad notes hung and lingered in the still morning air. The last note echoed down the valley as the ramrod straight captain dropped his salute and commanded "Or-der . . . arms!"

The villagers watching the simple ceremony were awe struck by these strange men who outwardly expressed their love for one another. Moira was crying . . . it could have been different.

Standing alone, with a light breeze blowing across the quiet burn, Brendan viewed his dead and expressed some doubt at his decision to fight." Come captain" Maelsechlainn said "do not regret your choice to fight, nor think of it as a vain pursuit. You chose amid doubts the path that seemed right: the choice was just, and it has been rewarded. For so we have met in time, who otherwise might have met too late.

Your journey through time has been marked by your given word. You fought for good not evil. You have a lot to be proud of."

*   *   *

Brendan had walked the battle area much of the day. Chieftains, nobles, freeman, slaves swarmed over the area arguing, and in some cases fighting. He chose to ignore the ogling of the naked women in ritualistic victory dances, admiring the Marines.

PART III

Famine

The third seal is opened and a black horse appears, its rider is holding a pair of scales in his hand, symbolizing Famine and economic depression. The scales are a symbol of death and famine.

Chapter Eleven

Cead Mile Failte

>If the heart of a man is depressed with cares
>The mist is dispelled when a woman appears.
>—John Gay, the Beggar's Opera

The sky was clear, the sun warm; the smell of human sweat mixed with the stench of animal manure and the aroma of roasting pigs and steers produced a strong, earthy odor. Usually a busy place, the castle simply bristled with activity. The guards had lifted the heavy bars of the doors and swung them slowly inwards as they grumbled on their great hinges. Tenants came and went all day. Many came only long enough to pay their rents; some stayed all day, wandering about the grounds, visiting with friends, taking refreshments. Moira blooming in yellow silk, and Mrs. Nolan, starched in white linen, flitted back and forth between the inside and the outside of the castle, overseeing several handmaidens who staggered to and fro under enormous platters of oatcake, fruitcake and other sweets.

Inside the castle of Maelsechlainn was the large assembly hall where the banquets would be served. Although it was autumn the weather had been colder and windier than usual. Against the chill a fire roared on the hall's central hearth stone. Yet there wasn't enough noise to drown out the clamor of a hall being prepared for a feast. The hall was long and wide and filled with shadows and half lights; mighty pillars up held its lofty roof. But here and there bright sunbeams fell in glimmering shafts from the eastern windows, high under the deep eaves. A gust of wind whistled into the big room's open door, blasting around the screen and across the hall with enough force to carry smoke from the hearth to the ceiling vent with nary a curl or swirl. Through the louver in the roof, above the thin wisps of issuing smoke, the sky showed pale and blue. The walls were decked with myrtle branches, yew and holly, and the fragrance of the evergreens rose up into the gallery, mingled with the smoke and fires and the harsh reek of men. Visitors could perceive that the floor was paved with stones of many hues; branching runes and strange devices intertwined beneath their feet. They could see that the pillars were richly carved, gleaming dully with gold and half-seen colors. It would not be long before Ireland's most gallant warriors would insult one another over the piece of the steer to which each would lay claim. For defensive reasons, the hall was built of stone and had a slate roof and narrow loop windows. Its door was a full story above the courtyard floor.

Tonight was plainly special; the young lad who played the pipes at the Great Hall had been augmented by two other pipers, one a man whose bearing and ivory-mounted pipes proclaimed him a master piper. The man nodded to the other two, and soon the hall was filled with the fierce drone of pipe music.

Brendan was in deep thought knowing that he would have to leave, yet surrounded by the peaceful castle and its surroundings and the cheerful company of the King and his knights, he somehow felt he had come home at last. Sensing that thought Maelsechlainn came up behind him.

"It's a fairly rich bit of ground, and there's decent fishing and a good patch of forest for hunting. It maybe supports sixty crofts, and the small village. Then there's the manor house, of course that's modern," Maelsechlainn said, with some pride.

Brendan glimpsed at Moira walking as she appeared to be floating or gliding along the ground in a most gratifying cloud of reverent admiration with bonfires as background and he abruptly stopped talking. His eyes covered her slowly from head to foot and returned to her face with a completely ungrudging nod of approval.

"Your majesty, I may want to take you up on that favor you offered me."

The King broke out laughing, as he saw the look the handsome young captain threw at his beautiful handmaid and slapped Brendan on the back "why of course; anytime."

* * *

How in the name of God did this happen? Brendan asked himself. A few days ago Brendan had been leading his company in counterinsurgency operations against the rebels in Columbia. He was now in an old Celtic castle in Ireland fighting Vikings!

One of the King's men had killed a deer that morning, and a portion of the fresh meat, cooked with turnips, onions, and whatever else he could find, would make a delicious dinner. Bursting with anticipation of food and contented, people were sprawled around the various great fires, listening to stories and songs.

Servants shouted to one another as they arranged the dinner tables; dogs yipped and chased the ends of white tablecloths as maids snapped them into place. Their raucous activity stirred the piney scent of rosemary that had been strewn into reeds covering the floor.

On the raised central hearth, a great fire now sent crackling swords of flames high into the air. King Maelsechlainn dressed in vivid blue wore a small crown for the occasion. A breath of stew-scented air flowed into the quiet hall, bringing with it the sound of folks at their meat. This was spiced by snatches of gentle conversation and the occasional thrill of warm laughter. Another time, the sounds would have been welcoming, comfortable sounds, but with Moira's life turned on her head, it seemed as alien as a foreign language.

Food was readily available, in the form of a modest feast, including wine, fresh bread, and roast beef.

Joseph Murphy

* * *

Late noon

Moira, who was sitting adjacent to the kitchen, looked up anxiously from her work; where she was preparing bread for the feast. She watched Brendan make his way through the crowd. She busied herself with the task at hand, and she folded her arms across her chest, several times, to stop trembling. Her stomach felt queasy, yet she felt light . . . . yes, she thought, delightfully light. A primrose yellow silk dress fitted her torso like a glove, with deep folds rolling back over the shoulders and falling behind in panels that flowed into the luxuriant drape of a full skirt. The sun started its descent in the sky, the wind freshened. She had intended to change her clothes earlier when the sun warmed, but the smells of roasting meat, coming from the assembly hall, reminded her that she was hungry.

She pretended to be startled when Brendan was standing before her.

"Cead mile Failte," she said. Her heart quivered with a little pang.

"What does that mean?"

"She looked at him, smiling wryly. "A hundred thousand welcomes." He was not yet thirty years old; a stranger from a different land and a different time but already a legend in this part of Ireland.

A bird called from a nearby tree, and another answered from somewhere behind where she stood.

Deep in the soul of Moira a tiny voice whispered,

"You are a fool Moira; you have fallen in love with this handsome stranger from a time not yet come."

A ward of the King could afford no illusions. She was worth much less than a single head of cattle. A wandering noble or even a common lout could amuse himself with her with no one to protest.

Brendan looked at the tiny smoothed skinned face which was somber in the bright moonlight. Darkness had arrived early this time of year; the long caressing evening of an Irish day. She looked like a river elf.

Smoke streamed from the kitchen complex and its many roof vents; what with feasting tonight. The wind filled with scents of stews, roasting meats, and baking bread.

"I told you I would be back. Will you walk with me?"

Walking with him was an experience like none she had ever experienced before. She had felt a need to be close to him and to feel his arms around her. And when he put his arm around her as they strolled, she had felt his warmth for her.

* * *

He marveled at the look of innocence on her pretty face. He turned his head slightly and tried to fix his eyes on the dull glow of the running river nearby as it responded eagerly to the moon's simmering rays. He watched the blue waters of Ireland's sacred river flowing calmly toward the Irish Sea. Had she really grown so much more lovely? Or was it merely the memory of a frightened half naked girl he had saved in the heat of battle? He began to feel shameful lust for her. It was powerful and insistent. How long had it been since he desired a woman? He turned back to look in admiration; his gaze turned instantly into feverish desire. Dinner was finished and her chores completed.

"You have lovely hair," said Brendan.

"What? This?" Moira raised a hand self consciously to her locks, which as usual, could be politely described as swirling curls.

He laughed.

"But it's so . . . curly," Moira said, blushing a little.

"Yes, of course." He looked surprised. "I heard one of Muirgel's handmaiden say to a friend at the castle that it would take three hours with the hot tongs to make hers look like that. She said she would like to scratch your eyes out for looking like that and not lifting a hand to do so."

Noise was beginning to come from the assembly hall. There would be wagers and arguments and of course, more drink. In a few hours, Moira knew, she would be the only sober Irish person in the surrounding land. The other wards of the King did not like her because she was puritanical; no drink, no frolicking with servant boys, no joking. She acted like a nun. The thought of loving someone had never entered her mind. At one time, she thought that someday she might love a man; she could hardly imagine its happening, much less a man loving her back; but now, strange feelings were running through her. She stood up facing Brendan and then slowly walked past him as the soft moon looked down in gentle reproach at she moved away from him toward the reedy banks of the river. Moonlight splashed the waters of the river as though someone had spilled a pitcher of milk.

* * *

"You small lassies clear off to your rooms right sharp," lady Nolan commanded. "If you'll not stay up there safe out of sight, you'd best scamper away to your own places. But no lingering in the corridors, nor peeping around the corners. There's not a man in the place who's not half in a bag already, and they'll be gone in an hour. "This is no place for lassies tonight."

* * *

The men in the Hall were rioting, dancing, and drinking, with no thought of control. No place for woman, Brendan agreed.

Outside, while parts of the world lay trapped in night's hold, the hall was as bright as day. Ensconced torches clung to the walls, each one sending up black tendrils of stinking oily smoke to stain the painted ceiling. Golden threads sparked from the weave of the embroidered fabric into panels covering the walls.

Close to the hall in certain sectors, flames from great bonfires ate away at the blackness of the night. The people of the Kingdom of Meath had herded their cattle between the fires, praying that the mating season would be fertile. The strong green logs carved and bound together began to glow. Laughter, song, the twanging noise of the lyres, rhythmic clapping of hands, the Dublin folks were whipping themselves into a frenzy. The autumn festival was much like a ritual excuse for the excess which the Irish seemed to need periodically in their lives.

*   *   *

The risk of Brendan letting these young folk think he was their savior was frightening. The fog in his head, due to recent events, was so thick he couldn't think straight. He followed Moira and they both walked a little distance away from the crowd to a spot where they could watch the moonlight on the bountiful fields of Meath. There they stood a long time next to one another content with that simple life, at peace in the mystery of that mystic land.

"You're quiet tonight, my brave captain."

"I didn't want to spoil the moment."

"Spoil what?"

"The feeling;"

"What feeling."

"The night air and you;"

"That's nice, Brendan Murphy. Thank you."

"It's an honor." Brendan was spellbound by her beauty as the glow of the flickering light danced over her body. He was afraid to avert his eyes for fear it was a dream and she would vanish in a blink. But then again this must be a dream; it can't be real.

"Well what do you think?"

"Uh . . . huh?"

"What do you think?"

He moved closer, drawn to her loveliness, wanting to touch the vision before him.

"Brendan?"

"You are ravishing Moira." The words came out in a trembling whisper

She looked up slowly, her blue eyes searching. "Not me. The table, the food, the wine, the celebration . . ."

With respect to romance, one never stops to think what underlies romance. Tragedy and terror, transmuted by time; add a little art in the telling and Wham a stirring romance, to make the blood run fast and maidens sigh. Moira's blood was running fast, all right, and never maiden sighed like she did.

One of the Irish warriors, with a little drink in him, approached him "Pity the poor man who finds the perfect woman and must live with her for the rest of his life."

They all laughed-even Moira, despite her scarlet face.

"Especially if the perfect woman is Irish," she retorted.

Brendan laughed along with her. It was peaceful with the river on their right flank and the fields of Meath on the left. It was a beautiful autumn evening, with air like cider and an evening sky so dark blue you could drown in it. They continued to walk slowly with that sort of absolute quiet that comes when you are some distance from any other person. The sort of quiet so hard to come by in his own more crowded time, when machines spread the influence of man, so that a single person could make as much noise as a crowd. The only sounds here were the stirrings of plants, the occasional shriek of a night-bird, and the soft thudding steps of horses.

How long had it been since he walked through the woods with a girl on a gorgeous evening with the smell of flowers in the air? He reached out and broke a clump of pine needles from the nearest tree, spreading them like a fan between thumb and fingers. The scent of the turpentine was suddenly sharper.

They paused, where he pressed the lightest kiss against her lips. It was clear that he intended only a brief and ceremonial touching of lips, but his mouth was soft and warm and Moira moved instinctively toward him.

She felt the bulk of his shoulders in her arms, the strength in his height as he cradled her to him. She buried her face against his chest. Yes, she was in love with him.

"I've held women in my arms before and kissed them, and . . . well" he waved a hand, dismissing the . . . *and*.

"It wasn't very pleasant indeed. It made my heart pound and my breath come short, and all that. But it wasn't at all as it is when I take you in my arms and kiss you." His eyes, Moira thought, were the color of lakes and skies, and as fathomless as either.

The Mystery of the Angels

He reached out and touched her lower lip, barely brushing the edge. "It starts out the same, but then, after a moment," he said, speaking softly, "suddenly, it's as though I've a living flame in my arms."

Brendan drank in the lines of her body with thirsty, piercing brown eyes. He curled his arms around her, and then lifted her chin with his thumb and forefinger to examine the depth of her immense blue eyes. He felt anguish, as though someone had pierced his body with a sword. He kissed her lips lightly, but she clung to him, demanding more. She turned it into a long wet, openmouthed kiss, the kind that would have stirred her had she any energy left in her body whatsoever.

Despite the myriad uncertainties of life here, despite the unpleasantness of the ill-wish, despite the small, constant ache of home, Brendan was in fact not unhappy; quite the contrary. He felt immediately ashamed and disloyal. How could he bring himself to be happy, when a whole Marine regiment must be demented with worry? Assuming that time was in fact continuing without him; he imagined the colonel going nuts over a missing Marine Company.

* * *

If Brendan used this private moment to once again rouse her senses, Moira wasn't sure she had the will to refuse him, not after several days of being tormented by the memory of his kiss on her ear.

Shivering, half in terror what she couldn't control and half in anticipation of feeling Brendan's flesh against her own, Moira backed as far from him as his grip on her arm allowed.

"Moira, I love you." The tenderness in his voice was overwhelming, and she leaned her head against his fatigue jacket, feeling his warmth and the strength of his arms around her.

"I love you too." They stood locked together for a moment, swaying slightly in the wind that swept down around them.

"What a greedy thing you are, my lady craving proof of my affection. Can you believe me now when I tell you that you are a treasure beyond any price to me?"

Rather than answer him, she rose onto her toes and touched her mouth to his, needing his kiss to know that this moment and he were both real.

They strolled back toward the castle, arms about each other. The whitewashed buildings leading to the main structure glowed amber against the bonfires and the moonlight. Instead of going into the main entrance Moira steered him up the slight rise behind the castle walls. Here they could see the whole of land laid out before them.

Chapter Twelve

Trojan horse

Who sows the wind, says scripture,
Must reap and reap again;
But he went out to sow the wind—
And reaped the bitter grain

—Captain Richard G. Hubler

Gunny Smith looked at Brendan and said "The good King thinks he has won a major victory, which he has but it is not permanent. Tuirgeis will regroup and be back. The Vikings are tenacious fighters and will never give up until either we or they are dead. We can keep killing them but they will keep coming; we have far superior weapons but they have more men then we have bullets, grenades and mortars combined. They are fierce folk when aroused. They will not give way now for dusk or dawn, until Dublin is taken, or they themselves are slain."

"What would you have me do gunny? We didn't choose to be here."

"Captain we started with 244 of the finest fighting men in the world. We are down to 28 effectives. We have 78 KIA's, 135 WIA's and 3 MIA's. At this rate we will become extinct. There are not enough men, not even if they were all gathered together and healed of their wounds and weariness, to carry the assault to Tuirgeis' stronghold."

"Go ahead."

"The Trojan horse"

"What?"

"The Trojan horse, in Greek legend, was a huge hollow wooden horse which enabled the Greeks to destroy Troy. Unable to capture the city after a siege of ten years, the Greeks resorted to stratagem; they sailed away and left the horse, filled with armed warriors, on the shore. A Greek spy persuaded the Trojans to take the horse into the city, convincing them that to do so would mysteriously make Troy invulnerable. That night the Greek spy let out the armed troops; killing the guards, they opened the gates to the returning Greeks, and the city was captured and burned."

"How do you propose we build a Trojan horse?"

"I don't but Maelsechlainn's daughter suggested we use the same stratagem. She said that these Genti's or heathens like their women. She suggested we infiltrate a Marine squad, disguised as maidens, in with numerous women of the night who visit our boy Tuirgeis. Once inside the compound they seek him out and WHAM, we snatch him or kill him. With the head cut off these other morons are sure to run. He's the key to their staying power. We take it away and they go poof!"

"How the hell do we get in without their knowing? The AO is full of people and base camps. How do we get in without everybody knowing we're there?"

The gunny leaned back and stretched. "At my request the micromechanical devices are making low-level passes over the site, as we speak, gaining intel."

"I see you assumed I would go along with this crazy scheme of yours."

"Yes sir; we have to go when the sun sets and hope to hell we don't get spotted until we get our man."

* * *

Moira's realization of Brendan's imminent departure, into harm's way, was deeply depressing. She suddenly realized just how much she looked forward to seeing him every day at dinner after the day's work, how much her heart would leap when she saw him unexpectedly at odd moments during the day, and how much she depended on his company and his solid reassuring presence amid the complexities of life in the castle, even if it all began just a short time ago. And, to be perfectly honest she realized how much she liked kissing him. The prospect of his absence was bleak and dangerous.

Strangely enough Brendan was not at all frightened now, though he had been unsettled by the plan. There was now only room in his heart for only one thought: it was kill or be killed. Therefore he was intent on doing the killing.

The sun was sinking behind the long western arm of the mountains when Brendan and five handpicked Marines, dressed as maidens, set out, with girls posing as prostitutes, for Tuirgeis' base camp.

* * *

The girls surrounded the five Marines; led by Brendan and Gunny Smith. It was a deep dark night by the time they reached the perimeter of Tuirgeis' base camp which was exactly where the micromechanical devices indicated it would be; beside the bend in a small tributary leading to the Liffey. The camp was silent and appeared empty as Tuirgeis' troops were sleeping; except for a few posted guards. The moon was gone as the mist or shadows blotted out everything like a great blanket all around them. Stars were shining above, but over the ground there crept a darkness blacker than the night itself.

"Stay where you are," whispered Brendan "wait until this mist passes us by."

The mist gathered about them. Above them a few stars still glimmered faintly; the air seemed warm and heavy for an autumn evening; and it was full of rustlings, creakings, amid murmur like voices passing in the dark. Long it seemed to them that they sat and were nervous but at last the complete blackness passed. They then were able to find their way with the Marines using their new modified night vision scopes; quickly making it past the guarded Viking outposts.

There was a great rumble of thunder away to the west, and flashes of lightning far across the valley floor. Inside the camp, a passing guard strayed too close to the girls and pierced the protective cordon. He immediately found himself looking into the deadly barrel of an M-16 with a silencer on it. The rifle spoke once and the guard slumped to the ground.

Every now and then the infiltrators could see mountain-peaks, miles and miles away, stab out suddenly, black and white, and then vanish. Behind them there were noises like thunder in the hills, but different. At time the whole valley echoed.

Dropping the Viking alone the route, as if he were drunk, the girls followed the path to Tuirgeis' tent only to find a pair of heathen soldiers waiting at the entrance of the approach to their chieftain's quarters. The guards were sitting in quiet watchfulness under a tree by the path, but they merely glanced at the girls. Apparently deciding they were no threat they went back to whittling at small objects in their hands. The moon was bright and the flicker of lights jumped off the leafy shadows. The girls quickly hunched their shoulders against the rain that started and made their way in silence now down the path to their destination.

The girls lured the guards close to them enabling the Marines to kill them silently. Once inside the tent they used silencers on Tuirgeis' private guard and clubbed the Viking leader into submission.

Upon leaving the tent a single screaming Viking came at them. O'Hare twisted around and fired his modified M-16. The Viking was propelled backward, contorted in midair, and fell heavily on his side. Suddenly the night air exploded with screaming Genti.

Another heathen soldier attacked O'Hare from the side as he instinctively reacted by bringing his right forearm down on O'Hare's shoulder and neck, sending him sprawling across the inside perimeter of the encampment. The Viking was on him in an instant, bringing his right arm around O'Hare's neck and jerking his head back with his left fist pressed hard into O'Hare's back. O'Hare managed to twist to his right and fire his hand sharply up into the Genti's groin; generating a noise and loosening his grip. O'Hare lunged backward, moving the man into the middle of the perimeter. With more room to maneuver, he drove his elbow into the heathen's chest. Now free, he spun around on his knees, and went straight for the face, thumbs finding the attacker's eyes. The pained scream reverberated through the grounds, as the hysterical girls fled for their lives. O'Hare stood, grabbed the front of the Viking's tunic and jerked him to his feet. He drove for the groin again, this time with his knee. The Viking slumped to the ground, his hands desperately trying to find the pain and make it go away. For a second O'Hare stood over him, chest heaving perspiration stinging his eyes. The Genti lunged suddenly for O'Hare's ankles but it was a feeble attempt. O'Hare quickly removed his Marine K-bar knife and moved it rapidly across the downed man's throat. There is something unnerving about a knife. Men who are fearless in personal combat will shrink from a naked blade. He looked up quickly with a quizzical look on his face when Golightly stoically said "We knew you could handle him without any help" as they quickly moved toward their preplanned escape route with their prized prisoner in tow.

The ground shuttered, the trees cracked and snapped, the air was split by deafening noise and filled with smoke and cordite. Hysterical men screamed, running everywhere, including the girls who slipped into the darkness. Leaves, branches, and wood chips fell like rain on the surrounding terrain.

Gunny Smith didn't see the two Vikings approaching him until the last second. There was no place to hide. The second Viking suddenly turned his head, as if he had seen something out of the corner of his eye. Smith lunged and swung the butt of his weapon, hitting the warrior in the head. The other Genti spun around. Smith unable to stop his forward momentum fell to the ground and rolled. He jumped to his feet and ran toward the heathen.

Golightly's knife had already made its deadly swipe as the gunny hit the falling body. Hot fluid spurted into the gunny's face, temporarily blinding him as he fought to break free of the lifeless body.

Golightly knelt by the warrior the gunny had hit and jerked his head up as he brought his knife around. There was no need; his neck had been broken by the blow. The front of his face above the eyebrow was grotesquely flattened.

Joseph Murphy

* * *

Struggle

Brendan took a deep breath, resolutely shoving aside thoughts of what might have gone wrong and concentrated on covering the rear of the small group of Marines and their prisoner as they fought their way out of the encampment, when he collided, full force, with a Genti rushing in. The man reeled backward, staggering with tiny running steps to keep his balance. Thrown off balance himself, Brendan crashed heavily into a horse-post, numbing his left side and banging his head. He clutched the post for support, the ringing in his ears chiming with the echoes of O'Hare's voice: "Get up, captain 'Get up!"

The Viking warrior, balance recovered, was staring at the young captain with his mouth agape. Abandoning the search for his M-16, Brendan stopped and drew his K-bar from his boot and continued upward with all the force he could muster. The knifepoint took the advancing warrior just under the chin as he reached for his belt. His hands rose halfway to his throat, then, with the look of surprise, he staggered back against a tree, and slid down it in slow motion, as the life drained away from him. He made the mistake of coming to investigate the commotion without bothering to draw his weapon first, and that small oversight had just cost him his life. The grace of God had saved Brendan from this mistake; he could afford no more. Feeling very groggy, he stepped over the twitching body, careful not to look.

Scrambling with his feet, pressing down with all his might, he pushed himself forward inch by inch, constantly straining to find and then pick up his weapon. It didn't take more than a few minutes to move those few feet, but it seemed he had been locked in battle with this grizzled warrior; whose head on collision caused him to be wobbly on his feet. Before he could move further he felt a stinging sensation on his right side. An arrow had pierced through the side of his protective vest and cut skin. Momentarily stunned another Viking was upon him. He had just enough time to maneuver the next attacker's body to allow him to get control of his weapon with both hands because he could never exert the necessary force with one.

He rolled abruptly away, and the Viking slithered at once into the small clear space between his body and his dead companion due to the force of the attack. Before the ancient warrior could rise to his feet, Brendan drove the rifle into his side, pinning him, however fleetingly against the ground. Brendan fired and the weapon jammed, without hesitation he lunged at his adversary and had both hands beneath his jaw now. The fingers of one hand were actually in the Viking's mouth. He could feel a crushing sting across his gloved knuckles, but ignored it as he forced the hairy head back, and back, and back again, using the angle of the dead Viking's body as a fulcrum for the lever of the attacker's body. He thought his arms would break, but this was his only chance.

There was no audible noise, but Brendan felt the reverberation through the whole body as the neck snapped. The straining limbs and the bladder at once relaxed. The intolerable strain on his arms now released, he dropped, as limp as the dying enemy warrior. He could feel the Viking's heart fibrillating beneath his cheek, the only part still capable of a death struggle.

* * *

Wounded

Brendan looked around to regroup his men but his body crumpled as his legs had given way altogether. He sat down with a thump, letting his shoulders sag and his head droop. Despair dragged at him like an anchor, pulling him down. Weapons fire and explosions could now be heard in the distance. He closed his eyes and retreated to some dim place within, where there was nothing but an aching gray blackness, and where the sound of voices and noise in general was no more than a faint yapping.

Brendan was seriously wounded. His field of vision contracted to a single dark spot, then disappeared altogether; leaving not darkness, but a bright void. He felt he was spinning or being pulled inside out.

He felt sick and dizzy. There was a confused noise of shouting nearby. It was the sound of human conflict. His eyes fluttered then closed. He woke with a start from a dream of endless winding stairs, with horror lurking at the bottom. Tiredness dragged at his back and his legs ached. He felt uneasy, isolated from his troops. What if they needed him? Worse, what if the Vikings did come, and find him? He rolled to one side and pressed his face against the cold dirt. The fighting and the explosions had stopped.

Brendan's hand twitched, then his eyes fluttered. Everything was in a dirty haze. He couldn't feel or hear. He was dying, he knew it. A hand grabbed his shoulder and pulled him backward.

"Move captain, move!"

Cpl Douglas Green, frantically pulling his captain toward a marshy ravine, fell, got to his feet, and yanked again. Finally he pulled Brendan through a small defilade protected by a fallen tree. He turned in time to see several Genti warriors coming at him with lowered spears. He immediately whirled and charged the onrushing attackers with his modified M-16 on full automatic. He cut them down like wheat but was hit with a crossbow, from the rear, in the back of the neck and pitched forward dead before he hit the ground.

* * *

In the fog of battle, O'Hare could not locate his skipper. He and his men had Tuirgeis, which was their objective, and he remembered his captain telling him if they got separated that the mission was of paramount importance. O'Hare being an audacious man, who would not hesitate to die for his company commander, a man of beetling brows, of ferocious language and a tongue as caustic as shaving cream, gave the command to move out with his prisoner. He had tears in his eyes.

* * *

Brendan's eyes opened slowly. He was in a trance. His body seemed to be floating, unable to right its awkward position. There were sounds, but they were behind the fog and far away. It was uncomfortable. He tried to reach out. Suddenly he was falling. . . . faster, faster and faster, unable to breathe. The fog cleared, revealing colors and loud sounds, but he continued to fall, faster and faster, as the sounds grew louder. Stop! Stop! His body jerked. He vomited.

 Brendan shut his eyes tightly in agony as his stomach convulsed and a warm, bloody substance flowed over his torn, exposed fatigue jacket. He opened his eyes, but he had to blink to make sure they were open. He stared into a spacious void so thick and dark, he felt relief at the sound of his own breath. He was on his side, looking at two large trees. His body seemed weighted now and it tingled. He turned slightly, letting the blood drool out to the already soaked ground. Feeling was coming back, as was the stabbing pain.

*   *   *

 Brendan lay in the bush listening to the Vikings running about, jabbering to each other. He was afraid they could hear his heart, it was pounding so loudly. Great retching waves of pain swept over his body, but he ground his teeth and kept silent. Sometimes a merciful blackness engulfed Brendan. He would pass out, returning to the agony of consciousness, pass out again. He could feel the blood oozing from his wounds, sense the strength leaving him. His thirst was a torment. Still he dared not move-not even after night had fallen, for the enemy was still active.

 Brendan opened his eyes once more. It was still and dark but the sounds outside were those of hell. He thought of the many nights he lay awake in a patrol base, looking up at the stars but never seeing them. His mind was always on the mission or his men; and tonight was no different. He grasped the tiny fins and yanked up. The small spear came out easily. The smell of death choked him as he lay on his back, conscious, but stunned. His body seemed heavy. The air was thick, making breathing difficult. He didn't feel pain right away but he knew he was wounded. He tried raising his head. It seemed too heavy. He closed his eyes. He then heard whispering and opened his eyes. He could barely make out the shape of giant tree trunks in the darkness. As he tried to get up slowly the pain rolled through his body. He'd heard people who suffered sudden pain say they saw stars, but he'd never experienced it himself, until now. The pain shot through his head; his brain felt as though it had been dislodged from its moorings. At the same time, the reality that he was about to die echoed inside his head.

The area was quiet except for the fires that were still burning and crackling. He once again fell off to sleep.

* * *

Moira sat at the entrance of Maelsechlainn's encampment watching the rain beat down on the muddy main road. She knew the rain would hurt Brendan's chances of making it back but she was completely convinced he would. She had willed it. Slowly quietly, her feelings for Brendan deepened. She had given him her soul with all its hidden places, strengths, and weaknesses. He would come back, and she was going to tell him again that she loved him. What else but love could it possibly be? It hurt too badly to be anything else.

* * *

Toward midnight Brendan's mind was wandering as in a dream, something to do with grassy fields and wildflowers, when he became aware that what he thought was a playful breeze tugging at his sleeve was a presence alongside of him; a pair of none-too-gentle hands. A hand came over his mouth. He stiffened in terror, and then relaxed to hear a voice whisper in his ear, "It's all right. It's me Gunny Smith." Shutting his eyes, Smith placed his hand over Brendan's and gently squeezed. Brendan smiled in the darkness and returned the squeeze. He closed his eyes and tried not to think of his pain. His side throbbed and his shoulder ached. Quietly he pulled at a corner of the sweat rag he wore around his neck and put a balled-up piece into his mouth. The pain came in small waves, and there was no way to be comfortable. Instead of squeezing Smith's hand, which he held loosely, he bit the cloth. Slowly gently Smith pulled Brendan away from the where he laid and into a thicket. He took off the wounded captain's shirt and tried to bind his wounds. But there was so much blood the shirt became soaked and was useless. Smithy threw it away. By dark, Brendan had lapsed into semi consciousness again, As Brendan's strength waned, it was all Smith could do to rouse him for sips of water that were keeping him alive. His lips were cracked and peeling and he could no longer talk, though he would still open glazed eyes when shaken roughly. His eyes stared fixedly, then gradually closed as he turned his head away, moaning softly.

Smith laid there with his skipper, through the night, through the entire next day, among swarming insects while the terrible sweet stench of decaying flesh rose from the lumps that had been their enemies, while their tongues swelled in their mouth, and while Brendan burned in the fire of his pain and Smith kept his hand clamped over his mouth to stifle groans.

"Listen to me. You have an arrowhead in you. It's gotta come out. I'm gonna cut a hole around the area and try to push it out, okay?"

Brendan nodded weakly.

"It's gonna hurt like hell. You better bite on your sweat rag," said Smith.

Brendan forced a smile. "Just like in the movies, huh?"

"By the way skipper we did real good. We turned Tuirgeis over to Maelsechlainn."

Smith moved Brendan's sweat rag to his mouth and leaned against him as he drew his knife. Brendan nodded to Smitty that he was ready. Smitty than made a quick incision and pushed with his thumb on the tip of the arrowhead. Brendan's arm and body were as taut as steel. Pus and clear fluid mixed with blood oozed out of the hole. Brendan bit on his sweat rag as tears streamed trickled down his cheek. Slowly, the arrowhead began to come out. Gunny re-bandaged the wound with the last clean bandages he had in his medical kit.

* * *

Iarnkne accepted, on behalf of his King, the prisoner Tuirgeis from O'Hare and inquired as to where Brendan and the gunny were. When he heard that they were in serious trouble he grabbed Tuirgeis by the nape of the neck and said "Yes, we will have peace," and then in a louder voice, "We will have peace, when you and all your evil works have perished. You are a corrupter of men's hearts and if anything happens to my friends you will die a thousand times over."

* * *

Brendan lay on the soft ground, exhausted. He was white and shaking with fatigue. He tried to spit. His tongue was too dry. He felt the way he had back in school when the coach ran him until he passed out. The coach kept asking him how he felt, trying to break him. He remembered he wouldn't give him the satisfaction of telling him he was tiring, and he kept running till he dropped. His body felt the same way now. His muscles seemed elongated and rubbery, and normal breathing was impossible.

At last it was night again and the retreating heathens had moved down river. Smith dragged him out of danger and finally to the Marine lines. He struggled to his feet, groaning as he did. His eyes were dry and hot and his throat ached, as though he was coming down with a fever as well. In fact, every muscle ached, his face stung, his head throbbed and then he collapsed.

"We got a live one here! Help me get him out."

* * *

Medical treatment

The sky was cold and damp, filling the horizon with a gray blankness that blended into the gray fog of the hills and the grimy cover of an early autumn snow, so that the castle seemed wrapped inside a ball of dirty cotton. Even inside the dark walls, late autumn's silence weighed in on the inhabitants. The chanting from the chapel was muted, and the thick stone walls seemed to absorb all sound, swaddling the bustle of daily activity.

Brendan slept for nearly two days, waking only to take a little broth. Once awake, he began to heal in the usual fashion of a normal healthy young man, suddenly deprived of the strength and independence usually taken for granted. In other words, he enjoyed the cosseting for approximately twenty-four hours and then became in turn restless even in a weakened state.

The cuts on his body ached. The scars on his limbs itched. He was sick of lying on his belly then his back. The room was too hot. His hands hurt. The smoke from the brazier made his eyes burn so that he could not see clearly. He was sick of broth.

She stood at the foot of the bed, watching him for a moment. The corpsmen and his private nurse recognized the symptoms of returning health, no matter how precarious, and were glad of them. The room was dimly lit by the glow of the brazier and by two enormous candlesticks, each nearly three feet tall, which stood on the table at the side of the room. The room was close and stuffy with smoke from the brazier. The only window was covered with a heavy tapestry, one showing men in battle with arrows in their torsos. She could only wonder afresh at how inappropriate this particular decoration was for a sickroom.

"Well captain how do you feel?" He shifted his eyes to the right without moving his head. A medic was looking at his bandages.

"Alive thank you," he whispered.

"The nurse who worked on you will be pleased with her work. Are you comfortable?" His eyes shifted up to the ceiling.

"Forgive my weakness, but it does hurt and I could use some painkillers."

Moira, standing behind the medic, smiled with tears in her eyes. She came around him to Brendan's side. For the first time he could see her without straining his eyes. She was very beautiful, he thought, as she moved closer and put one hand behind his neck and the other on his left shoulder. Her hands were soft and warm.

He lied patiently, not moving as Moira circled behind him and inspected his front and back. She didn't know how bad he thought it was, but it was bad enough. Even by candlelight she was appalled. Before she had seen only the shoulder but the wound covered almost his entire side and back from shoulders to waist; cutting across the smooth muscles. He had not only survived an arrow wound but several stab wounds. She thought with some regret that it must have been quite a beautiful torso at one time. His skin was fair and fresh, and the lines of bone and muscle were still solid and graceful, the shoulders flat and square-set and the backbone a smooth, straight groove cut deep between the rounded columns of muscle that rose on either side of it.

"You look wonderful, just wonderful." This was of course entirely untrue; shirtless, scarred and blood-smeared, with stubble cheeks and reddened eyelids from the long period out in the marsh, he looked thoroughly disreputable. The fire's flickering illumination pierced some of the torn bandages, silhouetting his lean form. Moira's heart skipped a beat. His bandaged top was slit nearly to the center of his torso. It was loose and felt open as he moved, revealing more than a glimpse of the powerful planes of his chest.

Dark spots stained the bandages on his shoulder and his heavily bandaged forearm. However, he had never looked more handsome or more alive to her. Moira's knees weakened. She would have fallen if Gunny Smith hadn't caught her by the arms.

"What would you have me do?" she inquired to the medic.

"Help me get these bandages off and we will clean the wounds and bind him again."

She slipped the harness off and carefully probed the shoulder joint. It was still swollen, with some bruising, but thankfully she could see no evidence of infection. She then pulled the bandages off as carefully as she could. Still they stuck to the flesh, coming away with a soft crackling of dried blood. Droplets of fresh blood oozed around the edge of his wounds, and she apologized for hurting him, though he hadn't moved or made a sound. He finally sighed deeply, but didn't move as she traced the deep scars, one by one, as though to show him the extent of the damage he couldn't see. She rested her hands at last lightly on his shoulders in silence, groping for words. She had tended warriors that were in battle before and she knew roughly what could be done for them. If there was time, and if they were the kind who talked to keep the dark at bay, you sat with them and listened. If they were silent, you touched them often in passing, and watched for the unguarded moment, when you might draw them outside of themselves and hold them while they exorcised their demons. If there was time; and if there wasn't then you plied them with whiskey, and hoped they would manage to find someone else to listen, while you passed on to a man whose wounds were visible. Brendan's eyes closed.

Brendan would talk to someone, sooner or later. There was time. But she hoped it would be her.

He was now uncovered to the waist, and she leaned forward to examine the wounds. It was a remarkable sight. Barely a hand's thickness separated the adhesions. She rubbed her eyes on her sleeve. He wouldn't thank me, she thought, for blubbering over his prostate form. She shifted her weight with a soft rustle of her skirts. His eyes opened at the sound, but did not seem particularly haunted. He gave her a smile, faint and tired, but a real one. She opened her mouth, and suddenly realized she had no idea what to say to him. His eyes fluttered.

Moira's gaze focused on his lips; never in all her life did she want to taste a man the way she wanted to taste him. All sense dissolved. She leaned toward him, her lips almost touching his when he drew a long, slow breath and opened his eyes.

"Am I not as sweet as the morning spring?" she whispered, and she gazed into his eyes pleadingly, and with imperious tenderness. There was no response.

She knelt quietly next to his bed, her eyes fixed on him. No one in history could have been more devoutly served as he was by this beautiful creature. The urge to feel his skin on hers demanded that Moira lean her head onto his chest. With all her might, she fought to hold back a watershed of tears. Brendan's hand fell back to his side. Disappointment was strong enough that she had to stifle her cry, the one that would have begged him to bring back his hand. Before she knew what she was doing; she lowered her head until his lips once again hovered about her ear. A tissue-thin veil, she was wearing, did nothing to stop sensation. Just as had happened when she was recovering from the assault his breath against her ear sent a desperate need to feel his lips on hers careening through her body. Longing exploded past Moira's ability to control it.

"I'm going to kiss you." She whispered. "I've waited long enough; I'll wait no longer captain, of Marines. You are a proud, arrogant, man; and Moira loves you."

It was the kiss of an inexperienced woman-hesitant and tentative. Her hand on his face was like the first light of dawn after a long, dark night. His strength was awakened. The pain was still great.

"That was nice. I think I'll do it again." Her lips this time were warmer, open, seeking his with passion. He didn't respond. He did not want to hope, he did not want the pain of returning life.

"I'm getting better, don't you think?" She said brightly. "I like taking advantage of you being wounded."

This time she lingered longer, demanding a response. Brendan's lips answered without his willing them to. Hunger leaped to hunger, passion to passion. "Wicked, lustful Marine," she said playfully, laying her head on his breast. His famished eyes were consuming her, he reached out to touch her. What a graceful neck. The birds were already singing a merry chorus; the air was filled with the sweet scent of autumn flowers. He clinched his fists to control his fingers which ached to touch her.

He was a good ten years older, much wiser and more experienced. He lusted after her and wanted her the way he wanted to breathe spring air. He had never really loved anyone before. Yes, he did have a special girl once. He really messed that one up. She had somehow gotten to him, but then he fought it. He said and did things to hurt her, and she left him. He remembered how her tears made him feel so helpless. He didn't know what to do or say. It tore him up inside and made him angry at his own weakness. He worked hard to drive her from his mind after that, but his heart still twisted at the thought of her. But Moira was different, and yet before today he didn't even know how to describe this feeling he had for her. Now in the crisp autumn sunlight, he knew.

"I'm not letting you get away, Moira," he whispered

"Why, because I'm your sun, your moon, your starlit sky?"

""Did I really say that drivel?"

"Yes. You said you loved me, too."

"Unbelievable! I remember nothing of that!"

"So you lied."

"No. I mean yes. I mean, I wasn't myself when I said that"

Moira laughed sarcastically. "Enchanted by the Fairies, I suppose. You were helpless against my spell!"

"Yes sort of."

He gave a quiet groan, and then caught her face between his hands. Touching her lips to his, he let his kiss tell her just how much she meant to him. Then breathing deeply, he released her lips and braced his forehead against hers.

A brisk kiss on his forehead and she was gone. Like a lotus, he thought, beautiful and delicate in the midst of a nightmare. Brendan sank back into unconsciousness. She stepped outside, and then gently closed the door.

When it was shut, she leaned her back against it. Muirgel stood a few feet from her, clinging to the house's side as she tried to find some relief from the rain under the short eaves. Moira looked at her and turned her face to the darkening sky. The rain had lightened these past moments but a strange cold mist was taking its place.

All Moira wanted was a warm private corner where she could rage, weep, and sleep for days without interruption. There was little chance of that. The mist grew stronger. At that moment a shadow fell over them. The bright sunlight seemed to be suddenly cut off. Both Moira and Muirgel cried out, and crouched, holding their arms above their heads, as if to ward off a blow from above: a blind fear and a deadly cold fell on them. Cowering they looked up. A vast mysterious mist had engulfed them.

*   *   *

Sweet dreams

Moira knew that there were two worlds, the ordinary land in which humans lived and the Land of the fairies in which the gods and goddesses, the demons, the fairies, and all the strange creatures which occasionally intruded into the lives where humans lived. The two worlds were not distinct but flowed alongside one another like a river passing its banks. Sometimes they blended together and humans went on adventures into the Land of the fairies. Other times the inhabitants of that world, not necessarily unfriendly, blundered into human lives.

Humans were better off if they had nothing to do with the inhabitants of Land of the fairies. Even those who meant no evil, like the fairies, could be dangerous through inattention or mistake. Sometimes even the fairies, who were the godlike folk that had ruled Ireland before the present inhabitants came, would take a fancy to a human and imprison him or her forever in their land of endless and pointless merriment. She shuttered and prayed that Brendan was not of that Land of the fairies.

Shock closed its hand around Moira, sapping the strength from her muscles and the life from her heart until she was numb from head to toe. She'd gambled on one man and lost all.

Moira closed her eyes. Oh Lord, she wasn't just besotted. Rightly or wrongly, she loved Brendan Murphy, captain of Marines, from the year 2005, from the Land of the Fairies.

* * *

Regimental Compound

Gunny Smith stepped from the jeep and walked straight to the ambulance. Two men were getting ready to lift a man lying on the ground onto a stretcher. Another held an IV bottle that was attached to the wounded Marine by a long, thin tube. Smitty moved closer, shielding his eyes from the glaring sun. He saw four other Marines lift the stretcher together and walk to the ambulance. Gunny walked beside the heavily bandaged captain. He was so pale. Christ! His eyes were half open, but only the whites showed. They lifted him gently and placed the stretcher in the metal rack.

"May I ride with him?" The black medic turned as he shut the door. "No, its . . . sure Gunny, hop in."

Somebody stuck a morphine needle into Brendan's arm. He closed his eyes. Sometime later he heard distant noises. The ambulance stopped for a moment and he found himself floating outside of his body where he could see marines all around him in bad shape. He could hear the groans of dying men. finally fatigue and morphine won. He dozed off to gray sleep.

* * *

Castle Meath

Moira ran her hand over the bed where she took care of Brendan and nursed him back to health. She dreamed every night about him and pictured them walking, hand in hand, along the river outside of Castle Meath, talking laughing and later cuddling up next to him. She lay down on the bed and she thought of his quick smile, his gentle touch, the way he laughed, and the funny way he held his head when he was angry. All of these images passed through her memory and spread a warmth through her that made him seem close. And then that day that the strange mist came and he was gone! They were all gone! How could that have happened? She had really believed they would make it regardless of the time warp.

* * *

Regimental Hospital

The nurse picked up a pair of stainless—steel scissors from the desk-top and poked them into her fatigue-shirt pocket, then patted her waist pocket and felt the stethoscope there. She turned when she heard the sound of the siren on the ambulance.

"We've got wounded coming in!"

* * *

He woke to the darkness of pain and fear. Somewhere in his brain there was a tiny light shining, a pinpoint of hope. He strove to blow it out. The light did not flicker. He blew harder. The light was unwavering. It seemed to grow brighter. Something broke inside him. It hurt to smile. Brendan's thoughts shifted to the blue eyed girl who had inexplicably torn at his feelings and left a hollow place in his heart. He hadn't thought of himself as a man who could be much affected by a woman he hardly knew, especially born in a different time zone. Yet, the blonde haired beauty with the gentle smile had gotten to him. He missed her. They had shared each other's hopes and dreams, and when they parted they felt closer than they had before he left. The thought of her lying beside him, of her body glistening in the candlelight, caused a warmth to spread through him and intensified the dull ache that ate at his heart.

* * *

Courtyard
Castle Meath

Moira looked up at Muirgel with puffy eyes. "Is there . . . . is there a chance, Muirgel?"

Muirgel shook her head sadly. "Time is against them, sweet Moira. No pun intended."

Moira stiffened and backed away from Muirgel. "Until I die, there's hope! There's still hope; it happened once it can happen again. Maybe I can go to him!"

* * *

Springtime

Fresh winds blew over the villages of Guada and Rawa, sweeping away the stench of death. Bright wildflowers sprang up on the crags and in the slate crevasses. New Shrubs and bushes bloomed. Clear springs welled up from deep underground to sweeten the caustic moat. Despite this revival, no one stayed either at Guada and Rawa. So dreadful were the memories, and so frightful would be the legends surrounding them, that the valley would never be inhabited again. Even when forests towered there and hawks soared, no roads would lead to Guada or Rawa, no hunters would venture close. In time the villages would be overgrown and crumble, what was left, to ruin. Nature would reclaim it once again.

Morning arrived. It rained early, and then the clouds were swept away by a cold, fresh wind. Ireland was beginning to turn its natural green. Moira emerged from her sleep. The cold wind stung her face. It felt good. She stretched her arms, drinking in the morning's clean air. Spring's birth was hard in Ireland. The wind coming up the Shannon whipped its waters into small waves against the current. There must have been a mighty storm on the Irish Sea.

* * *

She had been in a trance all day. The waters of the Irish Sea lapped quietly on the beach. Behind the large headland the moon had already set. Stars winked implacably at Moira. Salt and fish smells permeated the air.

PART IV

Death

The fourth seal is opened and a Pale horse appears whose rider is named death; and Hades rides with him. The color symbolizes fear, sickness, decay and death.

Chapter Thirteen

Return to the Present

"The future belongs to those who believe in the beauty of their dreams."

-Eleanor Roosevelt

Summer

The larches and alders were a deeper green, because it was now summer, not late spring. The flowers had changed from fragile pinks and whites of May blossom and violets to the warmer golds and yellows of gorse and broom. The sky above was a deeper blue, but the surface of the lake was the same; a flat blue-black that caught reflections from the bank above and held them trapped, colors muted under smoked glass.

* * *

"How are you feeling?"
"It feels as though it's healing well," he said trying to look sideways at the wound.

"It doesn't pain me much."

"That's good, the nurse said, clearing her throat of some obstruction that seemed to have lodged there. "It *is* healing well; it's scabbed over nicely, and there is no drainage at all. Just keep it clean, and don't use the arm and twist the body more than you must for another two or three days." She patted the undamaged shoulder, signifying dismissal. Brendan put his shirt back on without assistance and went back to his ward to lie down in his bed for a rest.

* * *

Regimental Hospital
Columbia

Brendan passed two medical doctors having an animated discussion.

"You should see Ireland! It is the most wonderful place; quaint villages, the green rolling hills with hidden valleys down below. Sheep dotting the pastures in the distance like tiny white balls of fluff. And the Air!—Ah it's as the world must have been over a thousand years ago. Clean—pure. Oh! I must not forget the people. They are amazing—so kind-so friendly."

Brendan fell onto his bed and quickly sank back into the misty trance that had numbed his feelings and clouded his thoughts on the voyage that he had taken. There was little joy in seeing some of his old friends, who were waiting for him, despite their joyous welcome. Poor Brendan had aged greatly; the rest of his men had been worn down by their journey like disabled veterans of wars long ago.

The nurse signaled they could go in.

How you doing, sir?" asked Smitty, leaning over the bed.

Brendan's eyes widened in recognition and he tried to sit up.

"Hold on there, Captain," said the attending nurse who quickly stepped in front of the visiting Marines and put a hand on Brendan's chest to push him back gently.

"You lie back and I will crank you up. I don't want you moving around too much.

"Smitty how is the Company?

The gunny could see the anxiety in his skipper's face.

"They are okay and getting healthier every passing day."

Brendan closed, then opened his eyes and looked at Smitty. "Were we dreaming?"

"No sir but I wonder if anyone else would ever believe us?"

O'Hare was about to say something when he heard Golightly say "attention"

Colonel Hull was approaching. "Relax men," he said coming up to the bed. "Brendan, how are you feeling?"

Brendan tried to raise himself up, but the colonel put his hand on Brendan's shoulder "Easy son. You have to get better first before you can run your company."

Brendan's eyes clouded. He was embarrassed at his show of emotion in front of his men.

"Son I want to thank you and your men for what you did in that valley. Nobody knows, or probably ever will, what you and your men did. You took on a whole FARC regiment in tight and up close with no room to maneuver. I am putting you in for the Silver Star with combat V. Well it looks like you have a lot of people wanting to say something to you; so I'll say goodbye."

The Colonel turned and left quickly. Some of Brendan's men waiting for him came into the room.

Brendan choked with emotion, was unable to speak for a moment.

"They claim we walked into a guerrilla ambush of epic proportions and turned the tide. Guada and Rawa villages could there be such places? There wasn't anything with that name on any map of Ireland ever. Even the Irish historians never heard of it. We lost so many men. How? Where? If those places didn't exist?"

"Captain, we were there," responded Smitty.

* * *

Henniger then began to tell stories to other patients and nurses who had gathered around. He had an inexhaustible fund of stories, about fairies, ghosts or evil spirits, and other inhabitants of Ireland, such as the leprechauns, being especially common at fords and crossings, though many lived in the deep woods.

The banshees were black shadow creatures that tracked a man, wailing in the night, foretelling his death." Henniger had his listeners spellbound. "The banshee, you see, is a death ghost. She howls and cries in the night when she comes for the souls of those about to depart this world."

"Gaelic folktales," Brendan muttered to himself.

"Heroes you know. Probably from Viking roots; there's a lot of the Viking influence in Ireland, and all the way up the coast to the west. Some of the place's names are Viking, you know, not Gaelic at all." Henniger continued.

"The Norsemen came down on that coast hundreds of times between A.D. 500 and 1300 or so," Henniger said looking dreamily at the horizon, seeing dragon ships in the wind-swept cloud. "Vikings you know. And they brought a lot of their own myths with them."

Brendan's mind wandered back in time and he could hear O'Hare's voice saying

"Back in our world we had hundreds of monsters; many of them from the movies, right? Well here in Ireland they have their banshees. They know the terrible wail they can make and know when to be afraid."

Outside the, the wind howled ominously. The banshees were abroad tonight. There would be a thunderstorm, prelude to a mighty storm that would come in a day or two.

Brendan closed his eyes and willed his hopes to go away. He slept, dreaming of a girl with golden hair. Her round blue eyes and bright smile blessed him. When he woke the next morning, he felt rested as if by dreamless sleep. For Brendan it was a dream; a succession of strange, unrelated images. He often did not know whether he was asleep or awake. Again friendly nurses came and washed him down and gave him clean garb to cover himself. Strength slowly returned, and along with it the strength to survive. Someone gave him a brisk kiss on the forehead and then she was gone. Brendan sank back into unconsciousness.

The Mystery of the Angels

* * *

Was the mist a door of some kind? And into what did it open? Was it an NDE (near death experience), where there was a separation from his body, a journey through a tunnel into a beautiful realm of light and love in where he saw all the events of his life replayed in great detail? There simply were no words for whatever it was. A crack through time, he supposed, because clearly he had been there, and the mist was the only connection. The eeriness of the mist had been overwhelming, but looking back he thought it was very similar to the fog of battle. Courage is in very short supply when there are mortar shells screaming overhead and bombs going off next to you. The kind of terror he had felt then was the closest thing to what he had felt when the mist enveloped them.

"For me, in that moment . . . ." Brendan paused, deep in thought, talking to himself. "It's as though time had stopped. All the humors of the body, all the blood and bile and vapors that make a man; it's as though just all at once all of them are working in perfect harmony; or as though they've stopped altogether." He often wondered whether that moment is the same as the moment of birth, or of death. He knew that its timing was different for each man . . . or woman he supposed. He went on talking to an empty room. "But just then, for that fraction of time, it seems as though all things were possible. One can look across the limitations of ones own life, and see that they are really nothing. In that moment when time stops, it is as though you know you could undertake any venture, complete it and come back to yourself, to find the world unchanged, and everything just as you left it a moment before. And it's though . . ." He hesitated for a moment his mind carefully choosing words.

"As though, knowing that everything is possible, suddenly nothing is necessary."

* * *

Looking up at the ceiling, he thought to himself that he would begin again the hopeless search for his queen with the yellow hair.

He strained to keep his eyes focused. Was she a magic princess or just a peasant girl?

* * *

Evening was falling, his eyes were fluttering.

"Could this have been a bad dream?" He thought to himself.

The nurse backed into his tiny cubicle by pulling back the drape; and prepared his pain killing shot. He could hardly keep his eyes open.

She prepared his arm for the shot.

"What is your name?" He whispered as he started into his deep sleep.

"Moira" replied the beautiful blonde nurse.

CHAPTER FOURTEEN

The Legend

> Thunder is good, thunder is impressive;
> But it is lightning that does the work.
> —Mark Twain

Tuirgeis' design included the supplanting of Christianity by the heathenism of his own country. When he captured Armagh, Ireland's Holy City he drove away "the followers of Saint Patrick," converted the church into a pagan temple and made himself high priest of the new religion. As if that sacrilege was not sufficient to arouse the special anger of the Irish he enthroned his wife Ota, upon the high altar of the principal church at Clonmacnois, the next most holy place in Ireland. From that sacred seat it is said she had given heathen oracles from the Clonmacnois altar. When he was finally captured through the stratagem of Muirgel, by the Marines disguised as maidens, and turned over to the King of Meath, he was drowned in Lough Owel, for the ravaging of Guada and Rawa.

It was said that after the death of Tuirgeis, Viking fought Viking along the east coast of Ireland and Olaf the White, emerged from the carnage as a small but strong and menacing kingdom. In the meantime, an Irish high king of courage and enterprise emerged, Aed Finnlaith, of the northern Ui Neill, and destroyed the Norse strongholds in the north of Ireland and followed this by defeating the Norse in a sea-battle on Lough Foyle in 867; then in a decisive engagement near Drogheda, his army carrying the Bachall Iosa and an enshrined relic of the True Cross, routed a mixed force of Norse and Irish. After this, no Viking settlements were reestablished north of Dublin and the brunt of the ravaging fell on middle and southern Ireland.

* * *

It remains a mystery to this day, as to how Maelsechlainn and a few thousand defenders beat an army almost six times its size at a village at the confluence of the Liffey and a small stream called the Poddle. The village had been founded at least two centuries earlier and was called, Ath Cliath, "the Ford of the Hurdles." It was also named Dubhlinn, "Blackpool," from the dark color of the water under the bog. Known as The Battle of the Liffey, in 837, there are numerous writings referring to strange people dubbed angels fighting with them. Thus many scholars refer to the battle as the 'Miracle or the Mystery of the Angels."

Epilogue

Joseph L. Galloway once said that there is no more responsible job in the United States Marine Corps than that of an Infantry Company commander in combat. The Marine Corps takes a 24 or 25 year old captain and puts him in direct charge of the lives of 244 grunts. The captain makes decisions daily, even hourly, that mean life or death to his grunts.

Although a work of fiction, I have been scrupulous in researching everything presented as fact in this book and at no time tried to change historical material.

Glossary of Terms

AO, Area of operation

Banshee, from bean sidhe, is a woman fairy or attendant spirit who follows the old families, and wails before a death. The keen, the funeral cry of the peasantry, is said to be an imitation of her cry. An omen which sometimes accompanies the old woman is an immense black coach, carrying a coffin and drawn by headless riders.

BIRD, Helicopter or plane

Charlie Mike, Continue the mission

Cobra, AH-1G Huey Helicopter Gunship—snake

Commo, communications

Doughnut Dollies, Red Cross girls

Extraction, Withdrawal of troops by air

Fire Team, consists of four Marines

Gunship, Armed Helicopter

Ireland, the very name is Norse in origin

KIA, Killed in Action

leanhaun shee, or fairy mistress, longs for the love of mortal men. If they refuse, she must be their slave; if they consent, they are hers, and can only escape by finding another to take her place. The fairy lives on their life, and they waste away, but death is no escape. She has become identified in political song and verse with the Gaelic Muse, for she gives inspiration to those whom she persecutes.

Leprechaun, or fairy shoemaker, is solitary, old, and bad tempered; the practical joker amongst the 'good people'. He is very rich because of his trade, and buries his pots of gold at the end of rainbows. He also takes many treasure crocks, buried in times of war, for his own. Many believe he is the de'Danaan god lugh, the god of arts and crafts, who degenerated in popular lore into the leprechaun.

Lurps, Long Range Recon Marines or lightweight freeze dried food packet

LZ, landing zone

M-16, Modified Rifle used by Marines, weighs 7.6 pounds

M-60, U.S. light machine gun, fired 7.6 rounds

M-79, Single shot 40 mm grenade launcher

MAV, Micromechanical flying insects, Micro air vehicles or micro mechanical flying drones

Medevac, Medical evacuation by helicopter

pook seems to be an animal spirit. Some authorities have linked it with a he—goat from puca or poc, the Gaelic for goat. Others maintain it is a forefather of Shakespeare's Puck in a *Midsummer Night's dream*. It lives in solitary mountain places and old ruins, and is of a nightmarish aspect. It is a November spirit, and often assumes the form of a stallion. The horse comes out of water. If you cannot, he will plunge in with his rider and tear him to pieces at the bottom.

Ruck, Rucksack, Backpack issued to Marines

Snakes, Cobra gun-ships

WIA, Wounded in action

END NOTES

Proper credit must be given to the following authors and their books for assistance in writing this book. In certain chapters sentences were taken from these books and I highly recommend them to those readers who want to travel back in time and dream.

Chapter 1

1. Wayland Drew, Willow p.203
2. Ibid p.21, 150
3. Diana Gabaldon, Outlander p.765
4. Ibid p.573
5. Ibid p.798
6. Ibid p.648

Chapter 2

1. Winston Groom, Shrouds of Glory, p.85
2. George Clark, Devil Dogs, p.102
3. Maire&Liam de Paor, Ireland p.132
4. Dinah McCall, Storm warning, p.124
5. Robert Leckie, Strong Men Armed p.35
6. Ibid, p. 37
7. Wayland Drew, Willow p.69
8. Ibid, p. 91,152,144,145,179

9. Ibid p. 202,209132,161, 163,164,165
10. Ibid, p.197
11. Andrew M. Greeley, The Magic Cup, p.53
12. Ibid p. 102, 103
13. Leonard Scott, Charlie Mike p.184
14. Ibid p. 293, 298, 300
15. Diana Gabaldon, Outlander p.675, 588
16. Ibid, p.732

Chapter 3

1. David Willis McCullough, Wars of the Irish Kings, p.121
2. Ibid, p.123
3. Ibid, p.127
4. Peter and Fiona Somerset Fry, A History of Ireland p.48
5. Maire&Liam de Paor, Ireland p.133
6. Ibid, p.133
7. Heather Graham, Night of the Blackbird, p.196
8. Ibid, p.197
9. Andrew M. Greeley, The Magic Cup, p.1
10. Robert Leckie, Strong Men Armed, p.40
11. Ibid, p. 46, 60, 61
12. Wayland Drew, Willow p.218
13. Andrew M. Greeley, The Magic Cup, p. 137
14. Wayland Drew, Willow p. 262
15. Diana Gabaldon, Outlander p.742
16. J.R.R. Tolkien, The Two Towers p. 114, 115

Chapter 4

1. Maire&Liam de Paor, Ireland p.135
2. Leonard Scott, Charlie Mike p.9, 241, 249
3. J.R.R. Tolkien, The Two Towers p.98, 127
4. Robert Leckie, Delivered From Evil, p.403, 407, 416
5. Johnnie M. Clark, No Better Way to Die p. 212, 233

Chapter 5

1. Catherina Day, Ireland, p.84
2. Maire&Liam de Paor, Ireland p.158
3. Peter and Fiona Somerset Fry, A History of Ireland p.60

Chapter 6

1. Maire&Liam de Paor, Ireland p.156

Chapter 7

1. Maire&Liam de Paor, Ireland p.160
2. Ibid, p.161
3. Andrew M. Greeley, The Magic Cup, p. 187
4. Diana Gabaldon, Outlander p.809
5. Ibid, p.567
6. Leonard B. Scott, Charlie Mike p.224

Chapter 8

1. Diana Gabaldon, Outlander p.757
2. Ibid, p.752
3. Leonard Scott, Charlie Mike p. 188, 245, 271
4. Ibid, p.245
5. J.R.R. Tolkien, The Two Towers p.120, 121, 128

Chapter 9

1. Andrew M. Greeley, The Magic Cup, p. 56, 57
2. Wayland Drew, Willow p.272, 273
3. Leonard Scott, Charlie Mike p.280, 282
4. Ibid, p.267

CHAPTER 10

1. J.R.R. Tolkien, The Two Towers, p.59
2. Ibid, 33
3. Leonard Scott, Charlie Mike p.246, 247

CHAPTER 11

1. Leonard Scott, Charlie Mike p.268, 269
2. J.R.R. Tolkien, The Two Towers p.123

CHAPTER 12

1. Leonard Scott, Charlie Mike p.284, 285
2. Ibid, p.270

CHAPTER 14

1. Seumas MacManus, The Story of the Irish Race p. 267-272

Glossary of terms

1. Catharina Day, Ireland, p.65
2. Catherina Day, Ireland 1995 The Globe Pequot Press, Saybrook Ct.
3. Maire&Liam dePaorc, Ireland 1958 Frederick A. Praeger, Inc.

A White Sport Coat And A Pink Carnation

The Incredible New Devilish Story

From
Joseph Murphy

***   Murphy links true events to capture the ideological, devilish, trusting, uncomplicated, lasting and always faithful friendships of high school seniors in the mid '50's;

***   Murphy takes the reader back to a time when religious education was memorization, intimidation and terrorization, the urban 1950's in America;

***   This book can be read on two levels. The first is the obvious story of a group of teenagers that are risqué, comical and eternally bound to one another. The other level is the ability of us all to triumph over injustice.

The aforementioned were actual write-ups about the book from either Barnes&Noble.com and or Amazon.com.

Now available in hardcover from Amazon.com, Barnes &Noble.com and Borders.com

DUTY HONOR COUNTRY

This Books Stirs Patriotism In Light Of Current Events

From
Joseph Murphy

*** A Bronx heart, a military soul, and a moment in time when country, family and valor were of primary importance.

*** Chronicles of Vietnam as well as intimate views of the life and times of young men in that period. Some times light, other times serious and historically accurate, the book leads you into the storyline with little effort.

The aforementioned were actual write-ups about the book from either Barnes&Noble.com and or Amazon.com.

Now available in hardcover from Amazon.com, Barnes &Noble.com and Borders.com

VALHALLA

Describes Heroism At Its Finest

*** This book is a must read . . . .
*** I've finished Valhalla and really, really enjoyed it. I know my Dad would like this book.

The aforementioned were actual write-ups about the book from either Barnes&Noble.com and or Amazon.com.

Now available in hardcover from Amazon.com, Barnes &Noble.com and Borders.com

Printed in the United Kingdom
by Lightning Source UK Ltd.
112979UKS00001B/33